I0666599

Quirks

First Edition

Published by The Nazca Plains Corporation
Las Vegas, Nevada
2007

ISBN: 978-1-934625-24-8

Published by

The Nazca Plains Corporation ®
4640 Paradise Rd, Suite 141
Las Vegas NV 89109-8000

© 2007 by The Nazca Plains Corporation. All rights reserved.
No part of this work may be reproduced or utilized in any form or by any means, electronic or mechanical, including photocopying, microfilm, and recording, or by any information storage and retrieval system, without permission in writing from the publisher. Printed in the United States of America.

PUBLISHER'S NOTE
Quirks is a work of fiction created wholly by *Christopher Trevor's* imagination. All characters are fictional and any resemblance to any persons living or deceased is purely by accident. No portion of this book reflects any real person or events.

Cover, Fleshblack Images
Art Director, Blake Stephens

Quirks

First Edition

Christopher Trevor

Contents

Introduction

My name is Christopher Trevor. If you are a constant reader of my work I thank you from the bottom of my heart and from the bottom of my socked feet for your support and belief in what I create in the erotic genre of literature. If you are new to my work and this is the first book of mine that you have picked up, I bid you welcome gentle reader. Over the last few years I have been fortunate enough to have thirteen books published, all of them featuring some kind of male oriented erotica or another. Discipline, erotic and kinky spanking, leather culture, bondage, tickling, uniforms and uniform worship and a host of other erotic venues seem to draw me like a moth to a flame. But for me the common denominator in most of my stories, (with the exception perhaps of my leather novel "Love Torture and Redemption) has always been men's feet, men's dress socks, men's shoes, men's boots, tickling men's feet and worshipping men's feet. Men's feet, as far as I am concerned should be considered one of the great wonders of the world. Over the years, and even before I became published I was writing fetish stories of this nature and I was also collecting stories from other like minded men out there. I kept those files and as Stephen King once said and entitled a book in the same fashion, "Everything's Eventual." I have chosen for this book some of my earlier stories, a story I CO-wrote with a buddy of mine, the classic "The Detour" and I have also included some letters, e-mails and correspondence that I had received from other fetish oriented guys out there. I have either changed the names on some of these tidbits to protect the person's identity, or, in some cases I did not include their name at all. Their names are not what matters, what matters are the tales they chose to share with me. What matters is that when it comes to fetish there are no two people alike. Each person has their own unique twist that they put on their fetish. Some men, like me will combine fetishes for a thoroughly erotic scene, bondage and spanking, bondage and socks, uniforms and tickling, whatever the mix, it all works well. Whereas, some men will only focus on one fetish, spanking for instance, for some of my buddies that I have chatted with overtime it's all about giving or receiving a good old fashioned ass thrashing. But whatever the fetish, whoever the players, as differently oriented as they may be, one thing remains the same, always play safe. Again, I thank you all from the bottom of my heart and the bottoms of my socked feet. And with all that in mind I offer you, "Christopher Trevor's Quirks and Erotic Eccentricities."

Note from a Reader: He really is like no other author. What he writes about will chill most men to the core, to their bones, to their soul, to their very essence. The first thing you notice about Christopher Trevor, physically that is, are his eyes. He has these very sad, very seductive looking eyes. But don't be fooled by that sad vulnerable look. He can see right through to your heart. He knows just how to use those eyes to see inside most men. The next thing you notice about him, upon sight, is that he has a very shy, very withdrawn type of look. It amazes most people upon meeting him that he writes what he writes. If you get to talk to him he comes off as a bit naïve sounding. I had read some of his works before I met him and had him sign a book of his for me at a leather event. It amazed me that this very laid back looking young man was "Christopher Trevor", the same person that wrote the riveting novel, "Love Torture and Redemption." But those eyes of his, my God, as I said, the first thing you notice about Christopher Trevor are his eyes… Something else you notice about him, if you get to meet him up close that is, is his scent. When I met him he was signing books, he was dressed not as a business executive this time, rather he was dressed in leather and he smelled GREAT. I bought a book from him and as he leaned down over the table to sign it I detected a scent of body lotion, something that he had obviously doused himself in, smelled sort of like coconuts…and the scent of the leather he was wearing mixed with it and mesmerized me as I stood there watching him sign the book for me. He's determined…the way he signed the book, the way his fingers grasped the pen…his fingers clenched that pen tight as he signed that book…

An Avid, Avid fan…

Quirks

"I work as a shoe repairman in a shoemaker shop," an anonymous guy said to me. "One time this really, really handsome thirty something year old executive walked into my shop with a medium sized bag with three pairs of his dress shoes in it. There was one pair of black lace-up wing tips, a pair of black lace-up cap toes and a pair of slip-on burgundy colored loafers. He placed all three pairs of his shoes on the counter and told me he wanted leather soles and new heels put on all of them. He was standing there looking real sharp in his suit, even at the end of the day the guy looked fresh as he would have in the morning. I tallied up his bill and handed him a copy of his receipt, telling him his shoes would be ready in three days. He thanked me, left a nice sized deposit and left my shop. As I slid my hand into two of his shoes (his wing tips to be precise) to place them behind my counter my fingers touched something really soft that seemed to be crammed into each shoe. What I pulled out of the shoes was a pair of the handsome executives black nylon dress socks, Gold Toe brand, OTC style to be exact. Now, I'm straight as a fucking arrow, but I got to admit that there was something driving me crazy as I held that handsome exec's socks in my hands. Obviously the guy had crammed his socks into the shoes after getting undressed in haste one night. Probably figured he would put the stinkers in the hamper the next morning. Maybe his wife was hot and ready for him huh bud? Fuck the socks; he just wanted to slide his sausage into her nice warm sweet bread. Come the next morning the exec completely forgot his socks were in his shoes. But he didn't forget that his shoes needed repairs. My nine-inch meat stick was hard as a rock in the grimy work pants I wear to the shoe repair shop. Making sure no one was in the shop and with my hand trembling I pressed the handsome executive's socks against my nose and mouth and inhaled the toe section of them heartily. The scent was euphoric to say the least. The socks were still kind of moist as well, which only added to the heady aroma emanating from them. The suited executive must have taken his socks off after having worn them for better than nine or ten hours at work and with the scent of his sweaty feet and the leather of his shoes still on them he crammed them into those wing tips. I inhaled again and the executive's feet stink filled my nostrils. My hard dick pressed against my under shorts in my pants. I pressed my crotch up against my counter and shot a load in my shorts the likes of which I hadn't experienced in quite a while, not even with the wife bud, not even with the wife."

"Three days later the handsome executive came back to my shoe repair shop to pick up his three pairs of shoes," the anonymous guy replied to me in an e-mail when I had asked him if he gave the executive his socks along with his repaired shoes. "When he walked into my shop and handed me his receipt I don't think he noticed his black socks hanging from a hook on the wall behind the counter. I've had them there ever since. Fuck man, whatever the hell it is, it drives me batty to have that exec's socks in my possession, on my wall, like a silly sort of decoration for a shoe repairman."

Reported to Christopher Trevor during an IM chat by a shoe repairman

"I was sitting by myself in a café during a midday work break sipping a latte' and reading the days New York Times Newspaper," yet another Internet buddy said to me after meeting me in the men's feet chat room. "As I sat there reading my paper and sipping my latte' I couldn't help noticing this thirty-something year old guy sitting nearby me who every few moments was stealing glances down at my feet. I politely smiled at him at one point and asked him if there was a problem. He said that there wasn't; adding that he was sorry for staring, but said that he really liked my socks. I was wearing black nylon ribbed calf length socks that dress down Friday with blue jeans and a cotton button down shirt with no tie. Glancing down I to looked at my socks and how my jeans were hiked up pretty far, giving the guy a good view of the socks he seemed to be totally enraptured by. With a quizzical look on my face I smiled at him and said, "Man, I don't even know what to say to that, but I will take it as a compliment I suppose." He said that I should and by that point my break time was over. I said good-bye to the guy wishing him a good day and hastily left the café. All day long I couldn't get that guy's compliment out of my mind. *He liked my socks???* I had been complimented on suits I was wearing, shirts, even my ties, but never had someone complimented me on my damned socks. During the workday, I found myself really sweating in those socks for some reason. When I arrived home that night I sat on the bed wearing just my briefs and my black socks, looking down at them on my feet, wiggling my toes. Looking at my socked feet made me wonder what the guy would want to do with my socked feet, if I gave him access to them that is. When my wife called to me that dinner was ready I was holding my socks in my hand. They were moist and kind of smelly from the long day. I didn't even remember taking them off my feet. My cock was rock hard in my briefs. I called to my wife that I was on my way to the table and tossed the socks in the hamper in the bathroom. Dressed in gym shorts and a tee shirt with a pair of slip-on canvas shoes on my feet I made my way to the dinner table. I didn't tell my wife about the guy in the café, but I do know that I will see him again. I've seen him there numerous times, but that day was the first time we ever spoke to each other, and the subject was my socks, of all things. I never had a sock fetish before, but that night when I went on line I searched out and found the male foot chat room.

Reported to Christopher Trevor during an IM chat by an anonymous buddy

"Man, am I tired, I hardly slept at all last night," the handsomer than handsome Afro American security guard said to me as he scanned me out at the checkpoint of the jewelry company I work for. "I'll be so glad when this day is over, that's for sure."

"Why didn't you sleep well?" I asked him with a grin as he finished scanning me. "Did your girlfriend keep you going all night?"

"Nah man, I live alone, that is I did up until last week," he said to me, putting down his electronic scanning device and facing me as I stood beside his post. "A buddy of mine gave me a puppy, a red nosed Pit bull to be exact."

"Ah, I see, and the dog barks all night," I said, thinking that was why the poor guy looked so tired.

"Huh, barks, I should be so fucking lucky," the security guard with the intense eyes said to me, his eyes seeming to pierce me. "Fucking dog licks my feet man, all the goddamned time, even when I'm trying to sleep."

"Your dog licks your feet?" I replied in astonishment. "Did you just say that your dog licks your feet?? You've got to be joking."

As a guy with a severe foot fetish I was suddenly transfixed by what this handsome Afro American security guard was telling me.

"I wish I was kidding man, I mean all right, sometimes it feels really nice," he went on, checking to see that no one was waiting to be scanned out of the high security area that he was presently posted at. "He really is such a cute puppy and all that, but God man, he licks my feet *all the fucking time, ever since I got him.*"

"Sounds like a dog with a foot fetish," I said, smiling.

"Hardy fucking har," the security guard replied sarcastically. "I don't mind it while I'm watching TV or talking on the phone, but when I'm trying to sleep it becomes a bit annoying, you know."

"Why don't you just keep your bedroom door closed so he can't get in?" I suggested.

"That's when he starts barking, yapping like you wouldn't believe," he said, shaking his head in disbelief. "He even scratches at the door till I let him in. Then when I'm back in bed the action starts, fucking puppy slobbers over my damned size eleven's bud. And let me tell you man, this puppy can go all fucking night at my feet. The other night it felt so calming that I just drifted off while he was lapping my arches. When I woke up he was still at it. But last night it worked in the reverse way man, fucking puppy kept me up practically all night."

"Maybe you can train him to leave your feet alone," I said.

"Yeah, and maybe I can't," the security guard said irritably as another employee of the jewelry company approached to be scanned out.

While the security guard scanned the employee we cut our conversation off for the moment. No need for someone else to hear of the handsome security guard's strange plight.

"There you go," the security guard said to the guy after he was done scanning him.

The guy walked off and I looked at the security guard.

"Have you considered getting rid of the dog?" I asked him.

"Yeah, sure I have, but as I said, it was a gift from a good buddy of mine," he replied. "And the puppy is so damned cute. If I get rid of him my buddy will be offended and think that I didn't appreciate the gift."

"What's the dog's name?" I asked.

"I call him Maximus, but I'm thinking about changing his name to Socks," the security guard said.

"Why Socks?" I asked laughingly.

"Because he really goes to town on my feet when I'm wearing my damned socks," the guard replied, sounding as if my question was a stupid one. "Like last night for instance it was kind of chilly so I left the navy blue socks that I'd been wearing with my uniform on. Man oh man that dog was under the covers at my feet and licking them in record time bud. Like I said, he kept at it all night and I hardly slept."

At the mention of the security guard's navy blue socks my heart pounded wildly in my chest.

"And I'll tell you something else man, my socks stink at the end of the day," he told me, sounding as if he trusted me with his most guarded secret. "I don't mean that they smell bad or that they have a slight odor, I mean, *my socks fucking stink!* My feet sweat like a son of a bitch, which is what really gets my damned socks stinking so much. And this puppy slobbers and licks 'em like they taste better than his damned dog food."

We both chuckled for a moment. He had to scan another employee before continuing.

"And it's not like it's something that he discovered either," he went on. "It started the first night I had him. It was my birthday and my best buddy came over with the box that the puppy was in. Being that it was a weeknight I was still in my security uniform when I opened the door, but I had my shoes off, you know. My buddy said that he wouldn't stay long, just that he wanted to give me my birthday gift. Well, needless to say I invited him in as he handed me the wrapped up box with the air holes in it."

"When you saw the air holes you must have known it was a dog or a cat," I said.

"Yeah, I suppose I did, plus I had been telling my buddy that I had been thinking about getting a dog at some point," the security guard replied. "I was surprised that the little guy didn't bark, being cooped up in that box and all. When I opened the box and saw that puppy I admit I fell in love instantly. I've always liked dogs."

We both smiled.

"Anyway, I picked the dog up out of the box, put him on the floor and in less than a few seconds he was licking the tops of my feet and wagging his tail at what looked like a hundred damn miles an hour," the security guard told me. "My buddy and I laughed and he said it sure looked like the puppy liked me, adding that he really liked my feet. We both watched as that puppy slobbered over and licked my damned socked feet like his life depended on it. My buddy even teased me, saying that it looked like he'd gotten me a dog with a damned foot fetish. Lucky me I thought. My buddy gave me a few cans of puppy food to get me started and I've been training the puppy ever since, you know, house breaking him and all that."

"Yeah, but you can't seem to train him away from your feet," I said.

"Naw man, it looks like I'm doomed to a life of having this damned puppy service my feet for me," the guard laughed. "He's even at 'em while I'm having dinner man. I mean, the other night I was sitting at the table eating, I was tired like you wouldn't believe, and the next thing I know that dog is under the table licking my socked feet. Fuck, he even flicks his tongue on my toes, tickles me a little you know. When I laugh he does it even more, shit."

"Well, if it's any consolation I have heard that dogs are very faithful to their masters and they show their affection by licking," I said.

"Yeah I know, but other people have their dogs lick their faces or their hands," the security guard said. "My damn dog licks my stinky feet, shit! Like I said, it's not like it's something that he became devoted to after he got to know me as his master. This was instant bud, as soon as he was out of the gift box he was at my feet."

Again we both smiled, something seeming to pass between us, a knowing if you would.

"One night last week I was on the phone with a girl that I've dated a couple of times," he went on. "While I was sitting there talking I had one leg crossed over the other, my socked foot dangling down. Well, needless to say that damned puppy went for the gusto bud."

"You mean he was licking your foot while you were talking on the phone?" I asked the guard.

"More than licking it man, that puppy was sucking my toes like they were a baby bottle," the security guard guffawed. "When I tried to shoo him away the girl I was talking to on the phone asked me what was going on, who I was talking to in my apartment. I told her that my damned puppy was busy licking my feet and sucking my toes through my socks while I was talking to her. And you know what man? Get this! She said that sounded so cute, so darling. Well, after she said that all I could do was look down at the puppy as he gnawed at my damned sock. He was licking my toes like his life depended on it or something. Now, *now* this girl that I've dated a few times likes to come over to my place and watch my puppy lick my feet."

"Are you serious?" I asked him in disbelief. "She comes over so that she can watch your dog lick and slobber at your feet?"

"Sure as shit man, the first time she saw it she thought it was just the cutest thing," he said, saying "the cutest thing" in a mock female sounding type of voice. "Then she came up with ideas and games to play with my feet and my puppy."

At that moment another employee came up to be scanned out. The security guard scanned the employee. I stood there waiting patiently to hear about the games and ideas that his girlfriend had come up with where his dog was concerned. God knows I was coming up with more than a few ideas of my own. When the security guard was done scanning the employee I asked him what kind of games his girlfriend came up with for him and his dog.

"Well, the first idea she had was to have me lie on the bed in just my socks while the puppy licked my feet and she jacked me off," he said softly, looking around to make sure no one was in earshot at that point. "I mean okay, I love having someone jack me off bud, what guy doesn't? But while a puppy is licking your feet??? And her game went even further. After I'd shot my wad she told me to simply lie still. While the puppy was licking my feet she got my socks off me and ordered the damned canine to now lick my bare feet. I tried telling her that he only really liked my feet while I had my socks on. But as I was telling her that she started jacking me off again bud. And I gotta tell you man, there was something really kinky feeling about being jacked off again so soon after I'd just shot my wad. And being that I was all sensitive and tingling the way the puppy was licking my bare feet felt thousands of times more intense."

Again we looked at each other with that knowing glance.

"And I'll tell you more bud," he went on. "I didn't come to work the next day because that girl spent the better part of that night jacking me off while my puppy licked my feet. A few times she put my socks back on me, man there was something *real fucking hot about that bud.* Fucking bitch puttin' my socks on for me, damn, then jacking me the fuck off over and over."

We both laughed and looked at each other again, this time a little longer than seemed necessary...

"I better get to lunch," I said with a grin. "But I do have an idea..."

"I'll bet you do bud," the security guard said and winked at me.

That night I was at the security guard's apartment. He was lying on his bed wearing just his navy blue dress socks, jacking himself off slowly while I knelt at the bed at his dangling socked feet. I was licking his big size eleven feet and sucking his toes like crazy while his puppy scratched at the closed bedroom door and yapped and barked like crazy, demanding to be let in.

"Yeah, yeah, you just stay out there and wait for later on!" the security guard grunted, lifting his head and smiling down at me.

He had his big black dick in hand and it was oozing and oozing pearly droplets of pre cum.

"Yeah, that's it bud, lick my feet, lick my smelly socked feet," he said to me and lay his back down. "Feels so fucking awesome. Shit, now besides that girlfriend of mine liking to play games with my socked feet I got you too bud. Who knows, maybe I will get rid of the puppy after all."

Author's Note: This quick story was inspired by an actual conversation I had at work recently with a security guard.

"Straight as I am, I have to admit that there's something about a (handsome) guy rubbing his socked feet on my face that gets me every time," a heterosexual guy in a M4MFEET chat room on the Internet said to me recently. "Especially if he's been wearing those socks all day in his dress shoes at his office job. Not to say that I would turn down a construction worker's hot socked feet on my face at the end of a long day of sweating in the sun."

Told to Christopher Trevor by an internet buddy while chatting

"There's a guy in my office who I always catch checking out my feet under my desk chair," Ryan, another supposedly straight guy said to me when he saw me in the men for men feet fetish chat room on the internet. "I never thought of my feet *or my socks* as erotic, but now when I get dressed for work every morning I can't help the strange feeling that courses through me, when I pull my dress socks on. I'm a suit and tie guy, so when I get dressed I put on my dress socks first then my underpants and then I stand there on my socked feet as I button up my dress shirt. It all used to seem so natural, so everyday. Now as I button that dress shirt I find myself wiggling my toes in my dress socks and my cock gets hard in my underpants."

Told to Christopher Trevor by an internet buddy while chatting

"Man, I forgot to pack a pair of thick white sweat socks in my gym bag," a suit guy said in the locker room to a buddy of his at the gym recently, as they were getting changed from their business suits to gym gear. "Looks like I'm going to have to work out in my damned black dress socks."

Conversation overheard by Christopher Trevor in the gym locker room

"I think that if I worked out in my dress socks rather than my thick whites it would make me feel very nervous, self conscious and vulnerable," a real sock fetishist named Dave, (Dave is married and also supposedly straight) said to me in an Internet chat. "Not to mention how those two buddies of mine would tease and razz me for it. More than likely they would say things like, hey buddy, what's up with the dorky black dress socks? Forget to pack your thick whites?"

Told to Christopher Trevor by an internet buddy while chatting.
Christopher Trevor and Dave shared lots of foot fetish tales, this was just
one of many things mentioned during their long line of chats

"Do you leave your dress socks on after getting out of your suit and changing into casual clothes when you get home from work?" I asked Dave in another of our Internet conversations.

"Yeah, I do leave my dress socks on after work," Dave replied, adding that his wife makes no mention of it.

Also told to Christopher Trevor by his buddy Dave while internet chatting.
Christopher added how the sock fetish seems to be more male driven than for
women, hence the fact that Dave's wife makes no mention of him leaving his
dress socks on after work when he changes to casual attire

The Detour

I was on my way home from a business meeting in Chicago. What a long and boring meeting it had been this time around, and all I could think about was getting home to my beautiful fiancée. My girl's name is Linda and we've been going together now for two years. I recently asked her to marry me and when I slid the marquis shaped diamond ring onto her finger she said, "yes" over and over through her tears of happiness. As I disembarked the plane I was also thinking how I couldn't wait to get out of this damned business suit. Some men call it a business suit. I prefer to call it a monkey suit. I was wearing a dark blue pinstriped Brook Brother's suit, a white button down shirt with a burgundy silk necktie, black Bostonian lace-up shoes and thin dark blue TNT sheer nylon socks on my size eleven feet. Like most guys out there I don't usually mention the color or style of my socks when describing what I am wearing, but, God almighty, for the purposes of this story my damned socks are paramount. When Linda gave me the sheer socks as a surprise gift that night I didn't think for a second the kind of trouble I would find myself in because of them, more on that soon, I promise. I'm just your average guy of five feet ten inches tall or so with blond hair and blue eyes. Granted size eleven feet are kind of big for a guy who's only five feet eleven but I consider myself blessed in that area, along with another very special area. I came down to the baggage area to get my one piece of luggage and saw a driver holding a sign that read, "Chris's Ride." He wasn't my usual driver but I did recall seeing him around waiting for other executives when they had disembarked their planes. He was a striking man; actually he looked like he'd stepped right out of a GQ magazine. He was about six feet tall or so with jet-black hair and dark sinister looking eyes. I could tell from the way he filled out his driver's uniform that he was more than muscular. I guessed his weight to be around one hundred and ninety five pounds. I didn't think that my ride would have been there already, but I was so relieved that he was since I was so drained from the meeting and the flight.

"I'm Chris," I said to him after retrieving my luggage from the carousel.

He just smiled, shook my hand and said, "You look like you're ready to sleep for a week. Bad business meeting?"

"Oh I sure am," I said as he took my luggage and we walked out to where he had a beautiful luxury van waiting. "And yeah, it was a long and boring meeting."

He placed my luggage in the back of the van then he opened the door to the back seat area and told me to hop in, to sit back and relax.

"Are you thirsty?" he asked me. "As you can see this vehicle is equipped with a full mini bar.

"Yes please," I said as he opened a started bottle of cold seltzer, poured a glass of it and handed it to me.

(A perfect gentleman he was.) It was a weird feeling let me tell you, that although I'm engaged to a beautiful woman I found the driver to be strangely attractive. Now I would never say that out loud, but I couldn't help but notice him. As I sat down in the back seat of the van he said, "Make yourself comfortable," so I propped my feet up on the consoles between the front seats. God, it felt so good to relax. I was starting to feel a little groggy and thought it was just the jet lag. Fuck me, but how wrong I was. I sipped the seltzer and watched as he hopped into the driver's seat and said, "Okay, we are out of here." I knew the trip from the airport to my house was going to be about twenty minutes so I just lay back to enjoy the ride, but little did I know what the driver had in store for me. And little did I know the "detour" my life was about to take.

"Nice socks," he said as he glanced down quickly at my feet.

"Thanks," I replied sheepishly, thinking what's so *good* about these socks.

I mean, I wear them all the time. I have a sock drawer filled with practically all the same style. I had never before had anyone compliment me on my damned socks. Suits, ties, even certain shirts I had worn I had received compliments on, but never my socks. My head was starting to feel funny by this time and as I sipped down the last of my seltzer he looked in the rearview mirror and asked, "Are you okay?" My head was spinning. I felt him start to slide his hand over my leg just over my shoes and again he said, "Nice socks." Jeez, I had no strength to pull my feet away so I simply said, "Get your hands off my feet please." I didn't want to be rude but his handling of my feet was making me uncomfortable. If he liked my socks so much I would tell him where he could go to buy them for himself, but oh man, it did feel nice as he moved his hand over my socked ankle up to my calf.

"Your fiancée must really think you're sexy in these socks doesn't she?" he asked me.

"Just drive and never mind my fiancée or my socks," I said sternly, wondering how he knew I had a fiancée.

I didn't recall telling him that I was engaged. I was starting to get agitated. I mean, what did he need to know for of how my fiancée feels seeing me in my sheer dress socks? My life is my own. He looked back again in the rearview mirror and said, "I bet your feet are nice and sensitive in these socks," and snapped the elastic in them against my skin. At that point I started to yell at him, "Get the fuck away from my feet man!!" The next thing I knew the van was stopped and he was grabbing my ankles. From the glove compartment he produced a roll of duct tape and secured my feet together and with one fast swoop he pulled me from the seat, wedging me down on the floor between the front and back seats. My feet were up on the console between the front seats and my body was jammed so tight that I couldn't move.

"Y-you put something in that drink, didn't you?" I asked him, feeling a tad more than nervous now, looking up stupidly at my duct taped feet.

It was the only explanation as to why I felt so weak and couldn't move. Fuck, I couldn't get away from him now if I tried, but I had to do something I thought. All he did was ignore me as I pleaded.

"Now this sure looks more than inviting," he said as he looked down at my shoes propped up on his console.

My eyes opened wider than ever in fear, seeing him reach over to the passenger seat and pulling a knife.

"Wh-what are you going to do with that?" I asked with tears in my eyes.

All I could think was, "My God, what is happening???" I watched in out-right horror as he slipped the knife under the laces of my expensive Bostonian shoes and started cutting my laces like they were butter.

"Here, let me make you more comfortable," he said sarcastically as he slipped one of my shoes off my feet. "Whoa, you must have been in these shoes a long time!"

He put my shoe to my nose and mouth and made me sniff the deep inside of it. The scent of leather and feet and sock sweat assaulted my nostrils. I have to admit that the smell was a bit overwhelming, even a little intoxicating. Now my sheer socked foot was totally exposed and vulnerable. Holding up one finger he smiled fiendishly and ran the tip of his finger across my sole. I flinched, trying to get away from his finger.

"Awwww, what's the matter, are you ticklish?" he asked me snidely, this time running the tip of his finger slowly across the bottom of my sheer socked foot, causing me to flinch again.

God, I am sooooo ticklish I thought, hoping that he was just being sarcastic. Thoughts of my fiancée tickling my feet and how much I hated it ran through my mind. She knows that when she tickles me she can get her way every time. Before I could even finish that train of thought though the driver's fingers were running up and down my sole at what felt like a hundred miles an hour. Fighting back the laughter was all I could do but the chuckling started anyway. I wanted to explode when he started in again, saying, "Coochee Coo, coochee coo as he was tickling my foot. The feeling of him running his finger over the bottom of my foot was getting me to laugh enough, but him saying "Coochee Coo" was making it all the worse.

"Ha, ha, ha, ha, ha, ha, ha, ha, ha, heeee, heeee, heeeee, sssssstttoooopppppp!!!!" I cackled crazily, laughing my laugh that my fiancée loves so much.

My foot twitched and wiggled, trying to get away from his relentless fingers. He then cut the laces on my other shoe with his knife and slipped that shoe off me as well. He reached down, placed my smelly shoes on my chest and forced me to inhale the scent emanating from them. Without skipping a beat he started in on my other foot.

"Heeeee, heeeee, heeeeee, ha, ha, ha, ha, ha, ha, ha, ha, ha!!!!" I squawked, laughing and crying at the same time and praying all the while that he would stop.

What a sight my feet were, wedged tight and shoeless between the console of this guy's van, and me too weak from whatever had been in that seltzer to move my feet from his grasp. Gawd, I was too weak to even move my arms to try to sit up and defend myself.

"What the fuck is going on!?!" I roared demandingly and all I heard in response was dead silence, dead silence except for the sounds of my hyena-like laugh.

All I could think was, "My God, I'm dead, what does he want with me? My socks of all things seemed to have caused him to go into a trance of some sort. He stopped tickling me and again drove the van. I lay there between the seats in silence, not wanting to distract him from driving, afraid to try to bring attention to myself, but mostly afraid that he would start in again tickling me. I looked around as we drove and didn't even recognize where I was at this point. All I wanted was to go home and sleep and now where the hell was I? Shit, what was going to happen to me? Fear gripped me like I was being squeezed motionless. I looked up at my captor in the rearview mirror. He had the most piercing dark eyes I had ever seen. Every so often he would look back and just smirk at me, teasing and tickling my feet as he drove, getting some good loud cackles and chuckles out of me. We had been traveling a ways and at that point I had no idea where we were.

"Oh, you are going to do just fine," he would say.

I looked up to the mirror again and he looked at me with such an intense stare that I could see he was planning something, formulating what he was going to do with me in his mind.

"Yes, you will do just fine," he said again.

I didn't like the way he would say that or the tone of his voice. He actually sounded like some sort of deranged or mad scientist.

"Why did I get in this van?" I asked myself.

When I saw that my usual driver wasn't there why didn't I not go with this guy? Why didn't I heed the warnings of the security chief where I work where traveling executives and the danger of abduction were concerned? Because I was tired, because I wanted to get home to my fiancée and most of all because I was horny, that's why, God!! I recalled the security chief telling us how kidnappers impersonated limo drivers in order to snag traveling executives for ransom from the companies they worked for. Although in my case I doubted this guy wanted ransom money in return for me. The way he was tickling me seemed to confirm that he had other plans for me. I started to thrash around a little, hoping I could get someone outside the van to notice my plight, and me but the windows were shut and tinted.

"Now be careful, you don't want to hurt yourself," he said with an evil grin, giving my socked toes a squeeze.

I didn't stop thrashing however. I knew that someone driving alongside us would have to notice my feet propped on his console. The front window wasn't tinted after all he had to see where he was going. And lets face it, how often does one see a guy driving with another guy's socked feet propped on his console?

"Why are you doing this to me?" I asked him in total fear. "What the fuck do you want?"

He looked back at me and said, "I've seen you before when you came back from other business trips and I've seen you sitting in the airport waiting for your ride. I couldn't help noticing you in these sheer socks that you wear while you were seated and I always wondered if you were ticklish."

Fuck, and fuck me hard bud, all this because he liked my socks??? I have an entire sock drawer full of them, SHIT!!! I could give them to him if that is what it would take to make him stop. My fiancée buys me my socks. Like most girls and most wives she keeps me well supplied in fresh pairs of socks and underwear. She buys me the sheer socks for a few reasons. First and foremost she knows that they're my favorites at this point, second she says that I look real cute in them, and third, and most important she knows how intense being tickled can feel while wearing sheers. But shit, it's one thing to have my fiancée tickling me, but to have this guy who had abducted me right out of the airport tickling me is a whole other story bud. After a long while more of driving he brought the van to an abrupt stop. He stepped out and opened the side door.

Reaching down he cuffed my hands behind me, still with that same evil look in his eyes. It was almost a playful look actually and I really didn't know what to think about it, other than the fact that I was in absolute terror when I heard him say, "Time to begin."

"*Time to begin what?*" I asked in more than total terror at that point. "What are you talking about? What do you want with me?"

By now tears were running freely down my cheeks. Again with that same response of silence he started to yank me roughly from the van and to over his shoulder, not letting my socked feet touch the ground. I could feel his hard muscled body as he effortlessly draped me over his shoulder and carried me toward the only house I could see around.

"Put me down!" I demanded angrily, my head dangling near his tight looking bubble butt. "Get your hands off me you fucking pervert!!"

I could still barely move, but I could feel that whatever he had slipped into the seltzer I had drank was starting to wear off, but damn, I was still going nowhere. All I could do was struggle in my captor's grasp, trying to wiggle and get away. But even if I did get out of his grasp where was I to go? I wasn't even sure where I was and I couldn't walk if he did put me down. As he got me inside the house he put me down but with my feet still secured with the duct tape and my hands still cuffed, God, as I said, I was going nowhere. I looked around the room and all I saw was a small table in the shadows with several things lain out on it. A machine or something was in another corner and a larger table suspended from the ceiling with three holes in it. As I looked around the room all I could think was, what was he going to do with me? I wiggled my toes nervously in my sheer socks.

"Please let me go man," I begged him. "I'll give you whatever you want, but please, just don't hurt me."

He finally spoke up in a deep voice saying, "I'll get whatever I want, don't worry."

Then, with fast agility and amazing strength he undid one of the handcuffs on my wrists, yanked my hands in front of me and quickly re-locked the cuff around my wrist. My hands were now locked in front of me. My God, as he had done that I hadn't even had the strength to resist him, he was that strong and that fast. Taking me by my hands he dragged me to the center of the room as I struggled uselessly, lifting them to the chains suspending the table he locked my hands into the chains. I could barely reach the floor.

"Now we can get down to business," he said with the most evil smile I had ever seen, yet there was something in his eyes that was almost hypnotic, so hypnotic that I was actually finding myself aroused.

He walked over to the table in the shadows and picked up a few items, looking at them in the way a surgeon would look at his instruments. I was terrified and aroused all at the same time, being tied up like this. What the hell was he doing and what the fuck was he going to do to me? He rolled the table over to me and I still had no idea what he was doing with all those things. Feathers, brushes, oil, a pen and the thing that frightened me the most, a large pair of scissors.

"You look so vulnerable hanging there like that," he said as he reached up and grabbed my ribs with his fingers.

I tried so hard not to laugh that sweat was forming on my forehead.

"What's the matter, cat got your tongue?" he taunted me.

"*Why are you doing this to me?*" I cried. "All of this just because you like my damned socks?? Jeez, of all things! Here, take them, they're yours, please man, and just let me go!!"

"Oh, I will have them when I'm done," he said. "But let you go? Hmmm, I don't think so."

Then he started to laugh.

"I've always wanted to take a young handsome suit guy like you and have my way with him," he said to me when he'd stopped laughing. "And when I heard on the dispatch radio that you were to be picked up from the airport I thought that this was a perfect time to try for you."

"Fuck man, I will give you whatever you want," I pleaded incoherently in fear at that point, glancing down at my sheer socked feet. "Here, take my socks, just let me go. I won't even call the police or anything, *just let me go!*"

As we were speaking back and forth he took the scissors from the table and started cutting away at my suit jacket.

"Oh GOD, *oh no, what the fuck?*" I garbled. "My suit, my suit is brand new, what the fuck are you doing man? Do you know how much this Brooks Brothers suit cost?"

But he ignored me again, giving me the silent treatment as he cut methodically and slowly. All I could think at that moment was my goddamned brand new suit and he's cutting it like it was an old rag. He looked deeply and intently into my eyes as he popped each button off my shirt slowly, one at a time. Slowly, so fucking slowly he cut away the rest of my shirt and off went my new tie with it as well. With his eyes riveted on mine he placed the scissors on the table next to us. Fuck, here I was all chained up and he started again running his fingers up and down my now naked sides.

"Ahhhhhhhhhhh!!!!! Ha, ha, ha, ha, ha, ha, ha, ha, ha, ha, ha, ha!!!!" I roared in laughter. "*Stop that, oh fuck, stop that!!! I am sooooooo ticklish!!! I can't take it, please doooooon't!!!!*"

"Stop?" he asked me, breaking his silence again. "What do you mean stop? I'm just getting started here."

He reached into my peach fuzzed blond pits with the tips of his fingers, wiggling them frantically.

"Ha, ha, ha, ha, ha, ha, ha, ha, ha, Noooooooo, *please not there!!!*" I laughed pleadingly, visions of my fiancée tickling my more than sensitive armpits fleeting through my head. "I can't take that!!!! Heeeee, heeee, heeeee, heeeeee, ha, ha, ha, ha, ha, ha, ha, ha!!!!!"

He was exploring my body with every wiggle of his fingers and it seemed as if he were taking notes in his mind, memorizing my most sensitive spots. I couldn't take it but I couldn't help that somehow it felt good too…

He stopped tickling me with his fingertips and my eyes then popped open wide in terror when I saw him reach into his pants pocket and he took out an electric high-powered toothbrush.

"Hooooo no, no," I blubbered as he flicked the toothbrush on to high speed, slowly bringing it toward me.

The bristles on that thing were vibrating at what looked like a thousand miles per hour. All I could do was watch in total horror as he moved it toward my armpits. When the bristles were pressed against one of my pits I nearly went crazy.

"Yaaahhhhhhhhhhhhhhhh!!!!! Ha, ha, ha, ha, ha, ha, ha, ha, ha, ha, ha, ha, ha, ha!!!!!" I guffawed. "Ohhhrrrr God, ohhhhhh fuucckkkk!!! Ha, ha, ha, ha, ha, ha, ha, ha, harrrr, harrrrr, harrrrrrrr!!!!"

"Hardy fucking har," my captor chuckled and spun the vibrating toothbrush around and around inside my armpit and then around the outer edges of it.

I couldn't even stop laughing long enough to catch my breath as he abandoned my first pit and moved the toothbrush to my other one.

"AYYYYYYYYYY!!!!" I cried out in laughter. "D-do you always carry a battery-powered toothbrush with you? Ha, ha, ha, ha, ha, ha, ha, ha, ha, ha, ha, ha, ha!!!!!"

"But of course," he replied as he tickle tortured my randy pit, pressing the vibrating device hard against the inside of my poor armpit. "One never knows when an opportunity like this one is going to present itself. And I truly do believe in good oral hygiene."

He spent a good twenty to thirty minutes alternating tickling my armpits with the toothbrush, listening to the music of my laughter it seemed. When he stopped tickling my armpits I felt a sudden rush of relief that was short lived. Short lived because the next thing he did was to start moving that damned toothbrush toward my nipples.

"No, *no, not my tits, please, oh please man,*" I pleaded to his seemingly deaf ears.

Looking down with an expression of more than dismay etched on my face I watched as he pressed the vibrating bristles against the very tip of my left nipple.

"AYYYYYRRRRRR!!!!!" I screamed and felt heat engulfing my nipple as he swirled the toothbrush over and around it, but really concentrating mostly on the tip of my poor nub.

"Seems that you have really sensitive tits eh?" he asked me, smiling meanly and fiendishly, giving my right nipple a squeeze as he tickle tortured my left one.

"AHHHHHHHHHH!!!! Ha, ha, ha, ha, ha, ha, ha, ha, ha, ha, ha, ha, ha, ha!!!!" I laughed loudly and bucked around as I hung there feeling totally helpless.

He switched to my right nipple with the toothbrush, and as he tickled that one and listened to me laugh I looked down at my left one. It looked like it was swollen up to twice its size.

"Ohhhhh my poor tits," I whimpered and laughed at the same time.

He stopped torturing my nipples with the toothbrush a little while later and the sound of it being turned off was music to my ears bud.

"We are going to have lots of fun here today," he said to me, pocketing the toothbrush.

Before I could catch my breath he went back to work cutting my suit off me, this time cutting away at my pants. When they were thoroughly cut down the sides he finally ripped them away, exposing a bulge in my underpants. I was hoping he wouldn't notice it.

"Awwwwww, you do like this don't you?" he asked, looking down, holding the shards of my suit pants in his hand.

I was more than mortified. Here I am engaged to the most beautiful woman in the world and somehow this handsome psychotic who had abducted me is arousing me. What would she say? What would she think if she saw me now in this more than fucked up position, stripped to my sheer socks and briefs and all chained up? How would she react if I told her that some guy had kidnapped me just to use me for his tickling pleasure *and, and because he liked my socks*. Looking at him again I had to admit he was quite stunning, broad shoulders, muscular arms and a chiseled body that couldn't be beat. All I could do was stare as he fell to his knees in front of me, looking at my bulge and jeez, sniffing my underpants. I had put on a new pair of Frederick's of Hollywood black silk bikini briefs this morning to surprise my girl with. She always said she loves the feel of silk and I thought for sure how these briefs would drive her crazy when she saw me in them. My God, of all the twisted turns of events, because now there was some guy staring at and sniffing them, *not her.*

"Oh, now these are nice," he said and started to kiss my cock through my underpants.

I started to moan, man it felt good. I couldn't believe that he was really turning me on now. Awwww man, fuck it, I got to admit, I wanted to shoot a load right then and there, *but this was a guy doing me, how humiliating at the same time!!* With his tongue and teeth he grabbed my silky briefs and slowly dragged them down, looking up into my eyes the whole time, my eyes that were filled with a mixture of fear and excitement at the same time. My big rock hard cock was now standing straight out, dripping big droplets of pre cum and my peach fuzzed balls hung low, sweaty, and smelly, in my sexy sac.

"Here, let me take care of that for you," he chuckled.

Sticking out his tongue he licked the head of my cock, cleaning off the pre cum. But every time he slurped away my oozing pre cum more of the good stuff would appear and he would lick that off as well. Man, I could not believe this that this guy had me wanting to cum so bad. This was beyond humiliating for a straight guy I thought. But nevertheless he went on and on licking my pre cum from the tip of my slit every time it appeared. I was jerked back to reality quite suddenly when he reached up to my armpits with his long muscular arms while he was sucking the tip of my cock. His fingers started moving frantically again against my pits.

"Oh Noooooooooo, pleeeeeeeasseeeee sttttopppppppp Don't dooooooo that!!!!" I cried out, but actually I wasn't sure if I wanted to laugh or moan in pleasure at this point.

He wrapped his lips around my cock and I have to admit that it got me even more excited. His fingers started to travel down my ribs and each time he touched a new area it would drive me crazy all over again.

"Ha, ha, ha, ha, ha, ha, ha, ha, ha, ha, ha, ha, ha, ha!!!!" I laughed crazily. "Coooooommmeeee on *sssstttttooopppppp!!!! I-I can't take this!!! Ha, ha, ha, ha, ha, ha, ha, ha, ha, ha!!!! No more please, nooooo more!!!!! Aaaaaaaaaaaaaha, ha, ha, ha, ha, ha, ha, ha, ha, ha, ha, ha!!!!!!*"

He then returned to one of the worst spots that he could have, my nipples, wiggling and twirling his fingertips over them, teasing them, grabbing them, tickling the fuck out of them.

After having tortured them with that damned battery powered toothbrush my poor nipples were beyond sensitive.

"*Noooooooo ohhhhhhhh Goooooddddddd, pleeeeeeaaase, not there, oh no, no, not there!!!!*" I reeled, trying to control my laughter as he tickled the worst place where he could have gotten me.

He looked up at me with those dark eyes and I felt what was akin to the most intense desire course through me. God, I must be crazy I thought he is so fucking attractive! But he's a guy. God, what would my fiancée say? How humiliating, *a guy turning me on?* He looked around the small table and reached to grab the oil. He doused my tickled and now more than sensitive nipples with the oil and I knew that with the oil on them his fingers were going to slide all the more. Moments later my fears were confirmed.

"Hee, hee, heee, heeeee, heeeee, heeeee, heeee, hee, hee, hee, ha, ha, ha, ha, ha, ha!!!! Ohhhhhh God noooo, heeee, heeee, heeee, heeeee, heeee, ha, ha, ha, ha, ha, ha, ha, heeeeee!!!!" I laughed that stupid hyena-sounding laugh of mine.

His fingers were sliding up and down my nipples, fuck, what could I do but laugh.

"G-get the fuck away from me!!!" I screamed at him. "*Get the fuck away!!!*"

Little good that did as he seemed to tickle me more and more the more I protested. I could feel the oil running down my chest. That in itself almost tickled the way it trickled slowly over me. It didn't help that my captor's fingers started following the oil down my chest, burrowing it into my thighs. Each inch was sheer torture. I thought I was going to go insane with his touch. Each second his hands were on me the closer I felt I was going over the edge. He slid his fingers over my throbbing cock. Oh please, let me just shoot my load I thought somewhat incoherently. It ached so bad that I just had to shoot, but now the fucker wouldn't even touch it. Gawd, first he sucks me up to a rock hard boner, tickles me in the spots sure to get me all worked up and more than horny and then he leaves me dripping pre cum, feeling frustrated and angry at the same time. Fuck, fuck, if my work buddies at the office could see me now I wondered what they would think. I wondered how they would feel if some deranged hunk had kidnapped them for their damned dress socks. God knows that all my office buddies wear dress socks…

I was jarred from my thoughts quite suddenly as my captor then grabbed my sheer socked feet by the ankles and flipped me over on the suspended table. THUMP, I landed stomach down atop the table. Immediately he yanked my feet and stretched my legs, fastening them to the table in a somewhat spread eagle position, positioning me then to fit in the three holes on the table. My cock and balls were pulled through the middle hole on the table and as well my nipples at the other end of the table were positioned in the other two holes. How lovely, I was a perfect fit. Now what the hell was I in for? Here I am I thought, spread eagle and face down on a table with my cock, balls and nipples sticking out on display beneath the table. Reaching down he then grabbed one of my feet and the brush from the smaller table next to us. Brush, brush, brush, brushing the bottom of my sheer socked foot. The way he'd started in on my sheer socked foot made me literally screech like a little girl.

"Sttttooppppp!!!!!" I cried, as that brush was a killer. "Heeeee, heeee, heeee, heeee, heeee, ha, ha, ha, ha, ha, ha, ha, ha, ha, ha!!!!!!"

I thought for sure that I was going to explode at that point. I could not believe that this fucker was so into tickling me.

"Get, oh God, get the fuck away from my feet man!!!" I managed to yell out. "Haven't you had enough already?"

Back again to the silence. He quickly undid the restraints on my feet and I could feel him slipping my sheer socks off my feet, the prizes he'd sought all along. He quickly fastened my now bare feet back to the table. Turning my head I saw him deposit my socks into a plastic zip-lock bag. No more, I can't take it I thought miserably as I saw him now moving that smaller table closer to us. I could see several feathers.

"Oh my God, what now?" I asked miserably, knowing all too well at that point why he'd taken my socks off me.

He pulled the first feather between my toes and with a wince I tried to pull away.

"No, no, you can't get away that easily," he said with a grin, breaking his silence for the moment.

He then explored the rest of my naked feet with that feather.

"AHHHHHHH, nooooooo, he, hee, hee, hee, heeee, heeeee, heeeee, ha, ha, ha, ha, ha, ha, ha, ha!!!!" I laughed uncontrollably. "Sssssstttttoooooppp nottttt thhhhheerrrrreeee!!! PLEEEEAAAASEEEEEEE!!!!!"

After a long while more he finally stopped and walked away. I was breathless. I thought that finally the ordeal was over and that he would let me go at this point. My cock throbbed big and hard pulled through the hole in the center of the table. What the fuck was going on with that? I must be crazy I thought. For no apparent reason this handsome guy had kidnapped me and was now tickle torturing the life out of me and somehow he was quite honestly turning me on. I can't be gay, I really cannot be. I'm going to be married soon and this is all insane. Looking at the small table next to me where he'd placed the plastic zip-lock bag with my socks in it. I thought what a shitty thing that was, to steal a guy's socks, of all things…

"Ha, ha, ha, ha, ha, ha, ha, ha, ha, ha, ha, ha, ha, ha, ha, ha, ha!!!! Heeeeee, heeee, heeee, heeee, heeeee!!!!" I roared laughingly as he was back at my feet again with that damned brush and brushing the bottoms of them, making them twitch in the restraints.

"Just want to have you really worked up for what I'm going to do to you next Chris," he said to me, calling me by my name for the first time throughout this whole twisted ordeal.

He stopped brushing my feet and then pulled over the machine that was in the shadows of the room. I had no idea what it was but I knew that now I was about to find out. I had never seen anything like it before that was for sure. There were three protruding feathers in the top center of the thing. They were in the shape of a triangle and fuck me tender but *they were rotating*. A few feet further down on the thing were three more feathers and just like the first three they were rotating as well. All I could do was lay there and watch in horror as he slid the machine under the table. I realized then that the feathers matched to the three holes (the two for my nipples and the other one for my poor cock and balls) in the table. He pushed a button on the machine and suddenly the feathers moved up higher and spun faster, spun faster against the very tip of my cock and over my dangling sexy balls and against the tips of my nipples.

"Heeeee, heeeee, heeeeee, heeeeee, heeee, heee, hahahahahhahahahhahahhahahhaaaahhhhhaaaa!!!!!" I blurted loudly and insanely as the machine under me did its evil work of tickle torturing the fuck out of me. "AAAAAAARGGGHGHhhhhh Noooooooooooooooooo Pllleeeeeaassseeeee stttttttoooppppppp!!!!!"

Now I knew why he had used that electric toothbrush on my nipples earlier. It was to get them all worked up and beyond sensitive for the torture he was now dealing them. I twitched and spasmed on that table like a fish out of water and as that devilish machine was tickling my nipples, cock and balls he went back down by my feet and started in on them. He tickled the bottoms of my feet with his fingertips while the horrid contraption under the table tortured me like crazy. I couldn't believe how the feathers working on my cock tickled and felt good at the same time. Never before had my fiancée tickled me in this type of fashion. God almighty, my fiancée I thought miserably, if she could see her man now. I knew that at any moment I was going to explode my executive juices. I felt my cock more than filled up and ready to empty out at any damned second. Amazing how being tickle tortured did this to me huh buds? Just before I was ready to lose my load he stopped the damned machine by reaching under the table and obviously flipping an "off" switch on the thing. The feathers stopped and receded back down into the machine.

"*God damn you!!!*" I yelled, knowing that he knew now that I wanted (needed?) to shoot my load. "*Gawd man, at least let me shoot!*"

He laughed at me and said that if he let me shoot my load he would set the timer and then flip on the tickle machine again under the table. Before I could utter a response he squatted at the side of the table, reached under it and grabbed my throbbing hard manhood. He started stroking it, making my balls swing back and forth in my sexy sac at the same time.

"Awwwwwwhhhhh yes, yes, let me shoot, *please let me shoot!!!*" I panted madly, my head raised up off the table, speaking through trembling lips. "Fucking kidnapper, goddamned hostage taker that you are, you got me so horned up that I can't believe it Mister!!"

"Heh, heh, the name is Wayne," he said to me as he stroked me faster, using the droplets of my pre cum as a lubricant over the crown of my manhood.

"W-wish I could say it's a pleasure to meet you Wayne," I garbled and then felt it. "But, ohhhhhhhrrrr G-god of gods, I-I-I'm goin' to cum man, *ohhhhrrrrr you fucking kidnapper, I'm goin' to cum like goddamned gangbusters!!!!*"

He stroked my cock for all he was worth and my head landed back on the table, as I was totally breathless.

"Ahhhhhhrrrrrrr fuccccckkk Wayne, Wayne," I gasped his name in the throes of forced ecstasy.

His hand felt like it was moving at more than a hundred miles an hour over my cock, siphoning every possible drop of the good stuff from me.

"Ayyyyrrrrrrrr fucker!!!" I seethed through clenched lips, lifted up my head again and quickly lay it back down.

I could imagine the mess my juices were making under the table as they splattered all over the floor each time he extracted more of the creamy stuff from me. When I was done shooting my cock went semi hard in his hand and he gave it a few last strokes, really sending chills and thrills through me at that point.

"Ahhhhhrrrrr fuck, man, I'm all sensitive and sexy feeling down there now Wayne," I gibbered stupidly, sweating like crazy. "Don't be strokin' my pud right after I've cum."

"I'll say you're sexy," he muttered and I heard the tickle machine under the table being moved back into place directly under my cock, balls and nipples.

"Oh no, no, you wouldn't man," I pleaded to his deaf ears.

Then, I heard a click as the machine was turned on and suddenly my now more than sensitive and sexy parts were being thoroughly tickled all over again.

"Ohhhhhhhhhhhhhhhhhh!!!!!! Hoooo, ho, ho, ho, ho, ho, ho, ho, ho!!!!!" I laughed, sounding like Santa Claus in ecstasy. "Ohhhhhhhrrr no, no man, not after I've just shot a monster-sized load."

"As I said Chris, I'm setting the timer," Wayne said to me, standing next to the table I was on, holding up a conventional cooking timer. "…to two hours…"

"T-*two hours????*" I squealed. "Ha, ha, ha, ha, ha, ha, ha, ha, ha, ha, ha, ha, ha, ha, ha!!!!!"

I felt the tips of the feathers under the table burrowing their way into the slit of my cock. I felt the tips of the other feathers spinning relentlessly against the tips of my nipples. I felt myself becoming hard again under the table and this bastard was going to make me wait two damned hours for the next explosion???

"Har, har, har, har, har, har, har, har, ha, ha, ha, ha, ha, ha, ha!!!!!" I laughed insanely. "W-Wayne, t-turn it off, please man, *turn it off!!!!*"

"Ah, but we had a deal did we not?" he asked me in a tormenting tone of voice. "I told you that if I let you shoot a load that I would set the timer."

"B-but, ha, ha, ha, ha, ha, ha, ha, ha, ha!!! But y-you didn't say I would have to be tickle tortured for an entire two hours!!!" I blubbered in between laughing. "Har, har, har, ha, ha, ha, ha, ha, ha, ha, ha!!!!!"

"Well, seeing as you're the sexy exec all tied up I would say it's *my* prerogative to determine how much tickling you will endure," he replied, ruffling my sweat sopped hair. "And after this two hours is over I'll give you a short break, and then it's on to another tickle marathon for you, possibly three hours."

"Ha, ha, ha, ha, ha, ha, ha, ha, ha, ha, ha, ha, ha, ha, ha, ha!!!!" I laughed and laughed. "Ohhhhh you fucker!"

Smiling meanly Wayne picked up a feather from the small table next to me and I craned my head to see what he was planning on using it for. And oh no, when I saw him looking at the crack of my spread ass I wished I hadn't looked.

"Ohhhhhhh no, no, th-that would be beyond awful Wayne, ha, ha, ha, ha, ha, ha, ha, ha, ha, ha, ha, ha!!!!!" I gasped.

Then, my eyes crossed in my head and I stared straight ahead in bewilderment and laughter as the guy slowly inserted the tip of the feather into my moist and sweaty rancid anus.

"AYYYYYYYRRRRRR HA, HA, HA, HA, HA, HA, HA, HA, no, no, ha, ha, ha, ha, ha, ha!!!!" was all I could sputter out as the guy twirled the tip of the feather in my poor anus, tickle torturing my rosebud. "Ha, ha, ha, ha, ha, ha, ha, ha, ha, ha, ha, ha, ha!!!!"

As the feathers on the machine under the table rotated at a high speed against my nipples, balls and cock tip Wayne twirled and spun the feather tip in my anus, driving me more than nutty with laughter. I farted loud and smelly a few times, which got my captor laughing as well and waving his hand around to clear the air. My butt cheeks twitched atop the table as Wayne managed to get that damned feather even further inside my hole, spinning it and twirling it as he went. I bucked madly and simply laughed louder and louder like a damned out of control hyena. My hands cuffed in front of me on the table pounded up and down involuntarily.

"W-Wayne, pl-please sssssstttooppppp!!!! Ha, ha, ha, ha, ha, ha, ha, ha, ha, ha, ha!!!!" I laughed and when he slowly extracted the feather from my twitching anal hole I farted loud, sounding like a buzz saw. "F-fucker!!!"

Smiling meanly he put the feather down next to me, stepped away from the table and picked up the plastic zip-lock bag containing my sheer socks. I watched, laughing all the while as the machine under the table tormented me as Wayne sat down on a nearby chair, holding my socks in hand like they were his prized possession.

"Wh-what is it about my socks, ha, ha, ha, ha, ha, th-that's got you so enraptured?" I managed to gasp in between bouts of laughter. "Ha, ha, ha, ha, ha, ha!!!!!"

Without a word the guy opened the zip-lock bag, took out one of my socks (his socks now) and pressed the toes section of it against his nose and mouth, inhaling deeply. He seemed to be in a state of ecstasy as he inhaled the scent emanating from my smelly socks. One thing my fiancée always complained about was how bad my socks smelled at the end of the day; even though she thought I looked really cute in sheers. Fuck, when I was a kid in high school I always wore thick white sweat socks with sneakers. Back then I never entertained thoughts of wearing dressy sheer socks, but when my girl told me how cute she thought I would look in them, well, my sock drawer became a collection of sheers bud.

"Ha, ha, ha, ha, ha, ha, ha, ha, ha, ha, ha, ha, ha, ha, ha!!!!!" I roared, watching as Wayne sniffed and even licked my stolen socks. "F-fucking pervert, sn-sniffing my rancid socks!!"

By now he had both my socks in his hand and was rubbing the toes section of them against his face, right under his nose, his tongue darting in and out of his mouth, stealing tastes of me on my socks. Watching him, laughing like crazy I felt my cock getting harder than hard under that damned table he had me lying on.

"Ha, ha, ha, ha, ha, ha, ha, ha, ha, ha, ha, ha, ha, ha!!!!" I cackled like a madman. "*Th-this is unbelievable man!!! Y-you got my socks, now, ha, ha, ha, ha, ha, ha, ha!!!! Now how about lettin' me go man???*"

"Let you go?" Wayne asked me. "But Chris, we're just getting started here. You can't go until I'm done with you."

"D-done with me? Y-you mean tickling me till I laugh myself to death?" I managed to sputter out before I was engulfed by another bout of violent laughter. "Har, har, har, har, har, har, har, har, ha, ha, ha, ha!!!!"

The feeling of the spinning feathers rotating against my wide sexy slit and over my balls and nipples admittedly was having a hardening effect on my most private member.

"Ayyyyrrrrrrrr, ha, ha, ha, ha, ha, ha, ha, c-can't believe I'm so fucking worked up again Wayne," I gasped, feeling my hard cock twitching slowly under the table, pre cum oozing at the tip of it.

"In need of some relief?" Wayne asked me teasingly, slipping my stolen socks back into the zip-lock bag and zipping it shut good and tight. "Mmmmm, need to preserve this great odor of yours. Now, what were we talking about?"

"W-Wayne, I'm so fucking worked up again under the table!! Ha, ha, ha, ha, ha, ha, ha, ha, ha, ha, ha, ha!!!"

"Ah, yes, need to shoot a second load my handsome young executive?" he asked me and stood up.

He stepped over to the table and picked up the feather.

"Ohhhhhh no, no, Wayne, don't do that man, come on, give a guy a break here!!!" I roared angrily as the guy again inserted the tip of the feather into my anal hole, rotating it as he went. "Ohhhhhrrrrr GAWD, y-you're goin' to have me fartin' and stinkin' up your place again man!! Ha, ha, ha, ha, ha, ha, ha, ha, ha, ha!!!! B-bastard!!!"

"Tell me how badly you need to shoot that second load Chris," Wayne teased me meanly, spinning and inserting the feather further into my hole.

"R-real bad man, y-your goddamned tickle feathers under the table have got me harder than a fucking rock!! Ha, ha, ha, ha, ha, ha, ha, ha, ha!!!!!" I railed at him.

"Are you sure it's the feathers that have you so worked up and not something else?" he asked me, looking directly into my eyes as I craned my neck around to look at him as he tickle tortured my butt hole.

I gulped hard and could only laugh in response to his obviously leading question.

"Does your fiancée get you this worked up Chris?" he asked me, sliding the feather around and around in my hole.

"O-of course she does, ha, ha, ha, ha, ha, ha, ha, ha, ha!!!!!" I responded. "What do you think, that I'm some kind of faggot like you? Ha, ha, ha, ha, ha, ha, ha, ha, ha!!!!!"

"Ah, now we're getting somewhere," Wayne chuckled and extracted the feather from my hole, getting some honking sounding farts from me.

"Arrrrrhhhhhh, ha, ha, ha, ha, ha, ha, ha, ha, ha, th-this is more than mortifying!!" I gurgled.

I pursed my lips tightly together and squeezed my eyes shut as more farts erupted from me and I was suddenly seized by another fit of laughter.

"Ha, ha, ha, ha, ha, ha, ha, ha, ha, ha, ha, ha, ha, ha!!!!!!" I laughed, my handsome captor watching that, with sadistic looking satisfaction as his feather machine under the table did its evil work, the feather held in his hand.

"Ha, ha, ha, ha, ha, ha, ha, ha, ha, ha, ha, ha, ha, ha!!!!!" I laughed and looked up to see Wayne standing at the head of the table.

"So many times I saw you sitting there at the airport waiting for your ride when I had been sent to pick up other passengers," he mused, running the tip of the feather over my face, up and down my cheeks. "So many times seeing you sitting there with your suit pants hiked up, showing off your sexy sheer socks."

I looked up at him and managed to grimace awkwardly.

"So many times I imagined having you here in this way, so many times I wondered how you would react to what I'm doing to you right now," he went on. "Let you go Chris? I think not, no, not for a while at least. Because as you can see I've waited too long to put this little plan of mine in motion."

"O-other passengers?" I blurted angrily. "Ha, ha, ha, ha, ha, ha, ha!!!! D-did you kidnap those guys too? Did you tickle torture them and steal their damned socks??? Ha, ha, ha, ha, ha, ha, ha, ha, ha, ha, ha!!!!!"

"Heh, no, none of them affected me in the way you did," he replied, looking around the room he had me trapped in. "You were the reason I created this whole setup Chris."

He ran the tip of the feather over my face a few more times and then stepped back to the center of the table. I nearly blanched and laughed louder and louder as the guy slid the feather into my anal crevice again...

"Ha, ha, ha, ha, ha, ha, ha, ha, ha, ha, ha, ha, ha!!!!" I laughed insanely, my cock beyond hard and throbbing now under the table. "W-Wayne pl-please man, ha, ha, ha, ha, ha, ha, ha, ha!!!!!"

"Still want to shoot that pent-up second load of yours Chris?"

Wayne asked me, sliding the feather in and out of my hole, spinning it in there every few seconds.

Chills and thrills coursed through my very being as I was past being sensitized at that point. It felt as if every part of my flesh was alive and tingling.

"I'll allow you to shoot a second load Chris," my captor said with a grin.

"Th-thank you man, thank you," I managed to grunt.

"After your two hours of being tickled are over," he said and slid the feather deep inside my hole.

"Ha, ha, ha, ha, ha, ha, ha, ha, ha, ha, ha, ha, ha, ha, ha!!!!! ARRRRRRRHHHH no, no man!!!" I cried.

"And you still have just about an hour and a half left to go my handsome young executive," Wayne chuckled, sounding real sinister at that point.

"Pl-please man," I panted, tears forming in my eyes at that point.

As much as I was laughing I have to admit I had never been so scared in my whole life... Admittedly, I cried like a baby in between my bouts of laughter... And, *and* I also should admit that I had never been so turned on before in my whole life. The hard-on I was sporting, and that was being tickled under the table was more than solid evidence, pardon the pun.

"I'll be back in a while Chris," Wayne said, taking the feather from my hole and placing it on the table next to the zip-lock bag that my socks were in. "I need to take care of a few things in the house."

"No, no, d-don't leave me like this man!!!" I roared at him, watching helplessly as he walked toward the door of the room.

"I'll bring you something to drink when I return," he said. "By the time your two hours of tickle torture are over I'm sure you'll need it."

Smiling, he waved at me in a feminine mannerism and then to my horror I was all-alone in that room, being tickled and tickled and tickled by that infernal machine under the table. My butt twitched and I farted loud and smelly... Two hours... *God!!!!*

Lying there feeling totally helpless, looking at the zip-lock bag with my socks in it I suddenly started thinking about the day my fiancée, Linda, had bought me those socks...

We had been dating for a good six or seven months when she gave me the small gift-wrapped box that she had in her night table drawer. We had just finished having some intense sex and we were lying side by side on her bed in her one bedroom apartment. Linda is five years older than I. She has beautiful long and silky brown hair, chestnut colored eyes and the body of a girl who jogs ten miles everyday, only because she jogs ten miles everyday.

"Feeling good?" she asked me, laying on her stomach and looking intently into my eyes in the softly lit bedroom. The light on her night table and the one on my side of the bed where the only lights on in the room.

"Oh, I'm feeling more than good," I replied with a smile as she gave one of my erect nipples a slight squeeze.

With my arms folded up behind my head I involuntarily flexed my biceps and pursed my lips as she'd squeezed my nipple. God knows my nipples are *always* sensitive and *always* erect after sex. Linda had noticed that early on in our relationship and took full advantage of it. Every time we were done having sex she loved to tweak and squeeze my nipples. She said I looked so cute when I grimaced at her touch.

"I'm feeling great," I said softly as she snuggled next to me and I slipped a muscular arm around her.

Laying there, both of us naked, our clothes strewn on the floor at the sides of the bed I gently kissed the top of her head.

"I love you," I whispered and my cock oozed what was left of my cum, dribbling at the tip.

Every time I told Linda I loved her it seemed to make my cock either pre cum or ooze more cum even after I'd achieved climax. She just had the effect on me, what can I say?

"I love you too Chris," she replied and slid out from under my arm. "I have a present for you."

"A present?" I asked her in reply as she reached over to the drawer in her night table and took out a small gift wrapped box. "But there's no occasion right now."

"So?" she asked me, holding out the box as I sat up on the bed. "We need an occasion to give a gift? It's something I saw and something that I've been thinking about for some time now. And I think we know each other well enough at this point to venture into some slightly kinky territory."

"Kinky territory huh?" I asked, holding up the box and shaking it, trying to determine from the sound inside it what it was.

Whatever was in the box sounded soft. That's the only way I could explain the sound it made.

"Open it Chris," Linda said with a grin.

"Sure thing," I said, leaning forward and kissing her on the lips before I got to the task of tearing into the navy blue wrapping paper.

She watched as I unwrapped the small box and then took the lid off it. With a smile of confusion etched on my face I took from the box one of three pairs of sheer calf length socks. The pair I was holding up was navy blue and ribbed. They are also the pair I was wearing when Wayne kidnapped me, the pair he now owns. The other two pairs were black and burgundy colored.

"Socks?" I asked her.

"Not just any socks, sheer socks," Linda said as I dangled the socks by their tops in front of my face.

"Yeah, so I see, sheers," I said, still not understanding. "You uh, don't like the socks I wear?"

"Well, like most guys out there you wear your socks till they're nearly decomposed," she said with a grin. "And I figured you could use some new pairs and a new style."

"I do not wear my socks till they're decomposed," I said with a sly grin, still holding the sheer navy blues in my hand.

I didn't want to admit that as soon as I had those socks in hand I felt more than a stirring in my cock. For some reason I knew I would be raring to go again very soon.

"Oh no?" Linda asked, reached down to the floor and picked up one of the cotton black socks I had worn with my suit that day to work.

Holding up my black sock she indicated the stretched material, the tear in the heel section and the hole where my big toe would be.

"See?" she asked me. "Decomfuckingposed! You wear such nice suits Chris. Your socks should be just as elegant."

We both laughed.

"Okay thanks, I guess I did need some new socks at that," I said.

"But sheers? Jeez, they look so frilly and feminine. And how are sheer socks going to take us into some kinky territory?"

"Put them on and I'll show you," Linda said.

"Put them on?" I asked her. "*Now?*"

"Yeah, now," she said.

"But my feet are all moist and smelly from wearing my other socks all day, the ones that you called decomposed," I said, sounding confused.

"Put them on," Linda repeated. "You're in for a treat."

"Okay babe, whatever turns you on," I said and leaned forward, rolling one sock first over my left foot and up to my calf followed by the other one.

Linda watched intently as I worked the socks onto my sweaty, moist and smelly feet.

"Gawd, I can smell my foot stink right through these things," I said with a grin, snapping the elastic against my calf. "But they do look kind of good on me don't you think?"

"Better than good," Linda said, running a hand over the tops of my feet and up to my calves. "They feel great too. I don't think you know it Chris, but you have very sexy feet. They're beautifully shaped and these socks really show the outline of them very vividly, not to mention *very* erotically."

"So now what?" I asked, not having mentioned the fact that my cock was again hard as a rock and as I said I was raring to go a second time.

"Now, lean back and grab the headboard at the sides," Linda instructed me. "And spread your legs out."

Looking at her with that uncertainty showing in my eyes I did as she said stretched myself out on my back and reached back to grab the sides of the headboard. My cock sticking straight up, twitching surely was a sight to behold. I was now stretched out in a spread eagle type of position and I have to admit I saw that Linda was looking at me adoringly.

"Okay, now no matter what, don't let go," Linda said and trailed the tip of one of her long fingernails against the bottom of my right sheer socked foot.

"H-hey, th-that tickles!!" I suddenly blurted as she held me by the ankle and tickled the bottom of my foot. "Ha, ha, ha, ha, ha!!!!"

"Hold still," Linda said and trailed her fingernail harder against the bottom of my foot.

"Wh-what are you doing babe?" I chuckled. "Ha, ha, ha, ha, ha, ha, ha, ha, ha, ha, ha, ha!!!!! Oh my God, y-you're tickling me…ha, ha, ha, ha, ha, ha, ha, ha, ha, ha!!!"

"And look at the effect it's having on you," Linda said with a smile, indicating my pre cum dripping hard-on.

I wasn't so sure that Linda tickling me was what was making me so hard. I was hard as a rock the second I touched those sheer socks. Now, wearing them, looking down at my big meaty feet in them and being tickled by the woman I loved was making me harder it seemed and not to mention how she had talked about my "sexy feet."

"Ha, ha, ha, ha, ha, ha, ha, ha, ha, ha, ha!!!!" I laughed louder, holding onto the headboard real tight as Linda tickled and tickled my foot, my cock twitching and my armpits sweating like crazy. "Ha, ha, ha, ha, ha, ha, ha, ha, ha, ha, ha!!!! C-c'mon babe, wh-what's the point of this?"

She quickly abandoned my right foot and moved over to my left foot.

"This one just as ticklish?" she asked me, grabbed me by the ankle and began tickle torturing the bottom of my left foot.

"OOOOOOO woooo yes, yes, it is, ha, ha, ha, ha, ha, ha, ha, ha, ha, ha, ha!!!!" I replied a fit of laughter seeming to engulf me.

Even though I wasn't tied to that headboard, and even though I could have stopped her at any moment I didn't. There was something so hot about the whole situation, wearing nothing but a pair of sheer socks, spread out like a Thanksgiving turkey, being tickled and harder than ever before all at the same time.

"Wait'll you see what I'm going to do after I'm done tickling you Chris," Linda said teasingly, looking hungrily at my cock.

"Ohhhhhhhhh, ha, ha, ha, ha, ha, ha, ha, ha, ha!!!!" I laughed, realizing what a lucky guy I was.

A while later Linda stopped tickling my feet and I was sitting propped up against the headboard as she lay between my legs sucking my big hard member. I was in a state of sweaty ecstasy to put it plainly. Every part of me was alive and tingling from having been tickled. Now, as Linda sucked me every part of me was more than alive. As Linda sucked me slowly, fast and then slowly again she ran her hands over and over my sheer socked feet, which were propped, at her sides. God, what was it about me wearing those sheers that so drove her crazy? And more importantly, what was it about them that so enticed Wayne to fucking kidnap my sorry and handsome ass??? Suddenly, I was jolted back to the present as Wayne came back into the room and juiced up the power on the machine under the table. I had lost all track of time at that point and I didn't know how long I had been alone in the room, alone with my thoughts of Linda. Now those rotating feathers felt like they were spinning at more than a hundred miles per hour.

"L-Linda, st-stop tickling me!!!" I suddenly blurted loudly as Wayne stood next to me, watching as I suffered in the throes of being tickle tortured.

"Were you far away and thinking about her just then?" Wayne asked me, ruffling my sweat-sopped hair. "When I came back in here you didn't even seem to notice me. You sure were laughing doubly loud though my young handsome executive."

"Y-you bastard!!!" I roared. "Wh-what is it that you and that fiancée of mine find so exciting about tickle torturing the fuck outa me?? Ha, ha, ha, ha, ha, ha, ha, ha, ha, ha, ha, ha!!!!! Ohhhhhrrrrrrr Gods almighty Wayne, turn the machine off, *please turn it off!!! Ha, ha, ha, ha, ha, ha, ha, ha, ha, ha, ha!!!!*"

I could actually feel the tip of the feather burrowing its way into my wide sexy piss slit, as if it had a mind of its own. I thought for sure that I would go crazier than crazy at any second.

I pounded my cuffed wrists on the tabletop.

"Turn it off?" Wayne asked me. "But Chris, you still have an hour to go."

"F-fuck man, ha, ha, ha, ha, ha, ha, ha, ha, ha, ha, ha, ha, ha!!!!" I laughed. "Th-this is really some fucked up shit here!!!"

My hard cock was twitching like mad under the table as those feathers did their diabolical work. My juice filled balls ached with the need to shoot that second load but I dared not ask Wayne to jack me off just yet. Fuck it all, I still had another hour of tickle torture to endure...

I squeezed my eyes shut and grimaced miserably, laughing like crazy as the feathers tickled my nipple tips, really sending chills and thrills through me at that point, mostly because my poor nipples were feeling pretty sore and numb at that point...

"Ohhhhhhhh God, I-I'm cumming babe!!!" I gasped in ecstasy, my mind returning to the night of sheer sock passion with Linda.

She squeezed one of my propped feet beside her real tight and sucked me down deeper into her mouth as I shot a whopper of a load.

"Ohhhhhrrrrr yeah, oh God!!!" I grunted in ecstasy, my head thrown back against the headboard.

It was the first time Linda had ever scoffed down my load and I have to admit that I was shocked and ecstatic at the same time. She gave my sensitive balls a few squeezes, getting the last of my good stuff to spurt from me. When I was done she looked up at me in that way that could always melt my heart.

"Guess what I want to do to you now," she said with a grin and squeezed my socked feet.

"Oh no," I whimpered breathlessly.

Without a word, it was as if I could read her mind I lay back on the bed and grabbed the sides of the headboard. Linda took my right foot in hand at the ankle and began again trailing her fingernail along the bottom of it, up and down.

"Damn Chris, your feet really do stink through these sheers that I gave you," Linda said with a giggle.

"Ha, ha, ha, ha, ha, ha, ha, ha, ha, ha, ha!!!! Y-yeah, I wonder why," I replied, laughing as well. "Jeez Linda, wonder how many of my office buddies have their girlfriends buy them sheer socks and tickle torture them."

"Only the lucky ones," Linda said and smiled at my semi hardness. "It's the silky material that the socks are made out of that make you that much more sensitive while being tickled. Somehow she knew that I would be hard again in no time...

Finally, *oh God, finally,* my two hours of tickle torture were over. Or should I say my first two hours of tickle torture were over. I was never as happy as when Wayne squatted under the table I was lashed to, turned off the tickle machine and pushed it away from my exposed nipples, cock and balls. The feeling of the feathers coming out of my piss slit sent a shiver through me. I glanced at that zip-lock bag that my socks were in and my harder than hard cock twitched under the table.

"Thirsty?" Wayne asked me, holding up a bottle of mineral water.

"Yeah, I sure am, but is that the same spiked shit you gave me to drink when I got in your van back at the airport?" I replied despondently.

"Heh, that's for me to know and for you to find out my handsome executive," Wayne said, taking the cap off the bottle.

Fuck, seeing as he wanted to tickle torture me some more I knew he wouldn't want me listless and sleepy. No, no way that was the stuff he gave me to drink back at the airport. Fuck it all, back at the airport. It seemed like forever since my capture at the hands of this lunatic. I lifted my head up as far as possible and Wayne held the tip of the bottle to my quivering lips, his other hand on the back of my sweat-sopped neck.

"Down the hatch," he said, inserting the tip of the bottle into my mouth.

After the first sip I realized how truly thirsty I was. With my eyes squeezed shut in ecstasy I slurped from that bottle like a nursing baby. I was more than thirsty. I guess being tickle tortured for two hours straight really can have that effect on a guy. When half the bottle of water was gone I began to feel a strange stirring in my cock. It was more than the twitching I usually feel when I'm really hard and worked up. The stirring sensation turned into a chill that moved through my cock and into my balls.

"More?" Wayne asked me, holding up the now half full bottle of water. (Was it water?)

I caught my breath and looked up at him.

"Yes please, I'm still thirsty," I stupidly replied and he eagerly slipped the bottle tip back between my lips.

This time as I drank the chilling sensation was suddenly in my very erect, very hard and very tickled and sore nipples. The way my cock, balls and nipples were hanging down through the holes in the table I was on made them all that much more sensitive for some reason. When there was just a drop of the water left Wayne took the bottle from my mouth and holding it up smiled meanly down at me.

"Ohhhhhhhh Gawd," I mumbled as my entire body broke out in goose bumps.

I could feel massive droplets of pre cum oozing from my wide piss slit at that point and I swear to God man, my balls were feeling as if they were twice their size in my sexy sac.

"W-Wayne," I said softly.

"How are you feeling now?" Wayne asked me, putting the bottle down on the small table next to me.

"I-I'm not sure man," I replied, squeezing my eyes shut and opening them wide, looking up at him with uncertainty showing in my expression. "Wh-what was in that water you just gave me?"

"It's a very powerful, very potent aphrodisiac from the orient," Wayne explained. "It contains potent vitamins and a mixture of herbs with just a dash of Viagra thrown in, hee, hee. The doctor who gave me the stuff said that a teaspoon of the stuff in a bottle of water is enough to keep a man overly horny and hard for hours. The bottle of water you just drank contained many teaspoons of the stuff."

I gulped hard and my cock oozed more pre cum, my poor balls and nipples churning like crazy.

"Ohhhhrrrrrr G-god man, y-you sick fuck," I blurted angrily. "Wh-what are you doin' to me here??? Shit, I feel sleazier than a whore does on a hot Saturday night when business is slow. Sh-shit man, y-you got to jack me off now!!!"

"Oh, I think that can wait for a while Chris," Wayne said teasingly. "After all you're not going anywhere any time soon."

"B-but, you said," I pleaded.

"You're the one stripped and tied up Chris," Wayne reminded me. "And speaking of stripped and tied up I want to hear about how your pretty fiancée tickle tortures you."

"N-no man, don't bring her into this, *please*," I panted every part of my body feeling more than alive at that point.

"Well, seeing as she was heavy on your mind just a little while ago I don't see how it's I who's bringing her into this," Wayne said. "Now, to avoid being tickle tortured for a little while more tell me about one of the times she tickle tortured you."

I looked up at him miserably.

Does she tie you up for it?" he asked me.

"O-one time she did," I replied, seeing no way out of this.

"Ah, then you must tell," Wayne said eagerly.

I took a deep breath, my skin crawling and began...

"I was staying at her apartment again, as we were seeing each other more and more often it seemed that I was there most of the time," I said to Wayne, doing my best to control the quivering in my voice. "Like other times when we had just finished having some intense sex we were lying side by side on her big queen-sized bed. She was totally naked and I was wearing a pair of black ribbed sheer socks, actually they were the socks I had worn to work with my suit that day. At that point in our relationship I was wearing sheers mostly every day with my suits. The only times I didn't wear sheers was on the weekends. But even on the weekends when we had sex Linda wanted me wearing sheers. She insisted how they made my feet look so much cuter, so much sexier and so much more vulnerable for her tickling pleasures."

As I spoke Wayne sat on the chair near the table I was on and once again had taken my socks from the zip-lock bag he had them in. As I spoke he held my socks to his nose and mouth and inhaled deeply my rancid foot scent.

"Man, I have a whole sock drawer filled with sheers at this point," I said to Linda as we lay there side by side catching our breath, basking in the afterglow as it's sometimes called.

"Heh, I wonder why," Linda giggled. "Seeing as I buy you a few pairs every payday. Now, for tonight I want us to try something new and even kinkier."

"Wow, even kinkier than me wearing sheer socks?" I laughingly replied, hoisting one of my feet off the bed and looking down at it, wiggling my toes.

"She wanted to tie you up," Wayne said, looking at me while holding my stolen socks in hand.

"Yeah, that she did," I said to him. "When she took the rope from under the bed I nearly grabbed my suit and ran. But when she looked at me so seductively I knew I couldn't deny her."

Wayne put my socks back in the zip-lock bag, stood up and walked to the end of the table where my cuffed hands rested, my arms stretched out in front of me.

"She tied me to the headboard at the wrists in a spread-eagle position and as she tied me I knew I was in for some devilish tickle torture," I said. "Fuck man, I was dreading it and loving the feeling all at the same time. How fucked up is that?"

"About the same as what you're enduring here," Wayne said with a grin and in what seemed like the bat of an eye he produced a long length of rope from under the table and quickly bound my cuffed wrists to the tabletop.

"H-hey, what are you up to now man?" I blurted at my captor. "Why are you tyin' my wrists down to the table? They're already cuffed and you've got my feet restrained too!!"

"I'm about to grant your wish, you're about to have an explosion like no other before in your young life my handsome executive," Wayne said, tying my wrists down good and tight. "I don't want you thrashing around at all once I get started on you. It's going to be an explosion the likes of which your fiancée could *never* wrest from you, no matter how much she tickle tortures you.'"

Without another word I watched as Wayne smeared some lubricant on his hands and fingers and then squatted down under the table I was atop of. I took a few deep breaths of anticipation and then felt a hand close around my erect shaft.

"OOOOOOOOO…" I swooned, my head bobbing up off the table involuntarily. "OOOOO God…"

Then, Wayne under the table and stroking my massive erection slowly, so slowly at first that it made my eyes cross in my head.

"Huhhhhhhhhh!!!" I gasped and lay my head back down.

I wanted to tell the guy to stroke me faster, but I was afraid that if I said a word he would suddenly stop working his hand magic on me. My body broke out in massive goose bumps as the guy stroked me a tad faster. I felt totally enslaved and in Wayne's power at that moment. Gawd, with the position I was in how else could I possibly feel. The lubricant on his hand and fingers seemed to be getting warmer as he stroked me faster. I guessed that it was one of those lubricants that heats up when it makes contact with human flesh. Suddenly I was breathless as I felt the guy's tongue swirling over my sweaty juicy balls and he stroked me faster still.

"Ohhhhhhrrrrr yeah," I muttered, looking at the plastic zip lock with my socks in it. "Fucking guy stole my damned socks right off my feet…"

Then, as he stroked me faster and tighter, the sounds of squishing filling my ears from under the table and as he licked and slurped my balls I felt the impending gusher starting. My balls seemed to spasm in my sexy sac and then my head popped up off the table like a jack-in-the-box totally out of control.

"Ohhhhhrrrrr fuccccckkkkk man, th-this is it you damned kidnapper!!!" I roared mightily.

My eyes again crossed in my head and seemed to roll back when I felt Wayne's lips encircle my shaft. He slurped my hardness deep into his mouth and I have to say it felt better than Linda's pussy. He started sucking me hard.

"Ohhhhhhrrrrrrrrr shiiiiittttt man, th-that damned Spanish fly you made me drink is working it's magic now you fucker!!!" I grunted and then the room was spinning as I shot a load like no other before in my life. "AYYYYYYYYRRRRRRRRR!!!!!!!!!"

It seemed to go on and on as Wayne sucked and suckled my spurting cock, draining my balls of my creamy juices, scoffing down my mess.

"Ohhhhhhhh f-fucking p-perv, eating my damned mess!!! N-never had some guy sucking my meat stick before, *God!!!*" I seethed in a mixture of ecstasy and revulsion.

When I was done it seemed like more than a few minutes later… God, it seemed like I had been shooting that load forever, longest one of my life bud. I felt as if it had been sucked out of me from my eyeballs all the way down through my cock. I felt my cock slip semi hard from Wayne's mouth. I could feel the last remnants of my sexy mess dribbling from my well-sucked member. I lay there catching my breath, but as soon as I was again breathing normally Wayne said that it was time to resume the business at hand. My feeling of ecstasy quickly turned to one of misery when I heard the tickle machine being moved back into place under the table.

"Ohhhh no, no, no more tickling me man," I pleaded to Wayne's ignoring ears.

Standing up straight again he looked at me quite quizzically, seeming to mull over my desperate plea.

"Hmmmm, perhaps there is a way you can avoid being tickled again so soon after shooting your load," my captor said fiendishly, rubbing the bulge he was now sporting in the crotch of his uniform pants.

"Yes, yes, whatever it is, just so I won't be tickled," I blubbered, not knowing what the hell he had in mind for me now.

Smiling, he again took my sheer socks out of the zip lock bag, but this time instead of sniffing them himself he pressed them against my nose and mouth.

"Take a good and long whiff of those socks of yours Chris," Wayne said, pressing them harder against my nose and mouth. "Smell yourself on those socks and see what it does to me."

I did as he said and saw that with his other hand he was still rubbing the bulge in his uniform trousers.

"I, uh, I suppose that tickle torturing me really got you all worked up huh man?" I asked him with a sneer. "Fucking perv, what're you going to do with that damned hard on huh?"

"Oh my tied up executive, it looks like I have to teach you everything," Wayne said, his words suddenly taking away my sarcastic attitude.

He slid my socks back into the zip lock bag and I watched as he pulled down the zipper on his pants. I gulped hard as he propped himself at the head of the table I was on, his long legs dangling off the sides of it, his huge meat stick staring me in the face. I stole a glance down at one of his dangling feet and knew what I would see, that he was wearing (black) sheer socks with his uniform.

"W-Wayne, no, no man, I'm no faggot," I panted, my lips grazing the tip of his big cock as it oozed pre cum.

"Okay then, then its back to being tickled," Wayne said and as he was about to climb off the table I hastily slurped his muscle pipe into my mouth, tightening my lips on it as he had done with mine.

Sitting across my restrained arms the guy moaned in sudden ecstasy as I slurped and sucked his cock for all I was worth. Under the table my cock twitched long and hard as I tasted Wayne's pre cum as it slid down my throat.

"ohhhhhhhhh,"Wayne groaned happily, tweaking his nipples under his dress shirt and I bobbed my head up and down, my eyes squeezed shut real tight as I suckled his cock. "Getting close already my handsome executive."

He grabbed the zip lock bag with my socks in it, took the socks out and pressed them against his nose and mouth as he erupted, jamming his cock still further down in my craw.

"Ohhhhhhrrrr yeah, fucking A!!!" my captor grunted as he spewed his mess in my mouth and down my throat.

I found myself sucking him more and more heartily as he seemed to cum and cum...

When he was done he slowly let his semi hardness slip from my mouth, sliding my socks back into the zip lock bag again.

"G-guess you drank some of the Spanish fly too eh?" I asked him, looking up at him as he climbed down off the table. "You sure shot a big load."

His only reply was to ruffle my hair and then squat down under the table. He clicked the feather machine back on again...

"No, no, ohhhhhhhhhh fuck, ha, ha, ha, ha, ha, ha, ha, ha, ha, ha!!!!!" I again laughed raucously. "W-Wayne, you said that if I sucked cock you wouldn't tickle me anymore!!! Oh jeez man!!!! Ha, ha, ha, ha, ha, ha!!! I even swallowed your damned mess man!! Ohhhhhrrrr fuckkkk, bein' tickled all over again!!"

"I said that you could avoid being tickled again so soon," Wayne said, correcting me, packing himself back into his uniform pants as he spoke. "Besides, who's tied up here? I'm the one in charge Chris..."

We looked into each other's eyes (adoringly) for a long moment...

"Three hours Chris," Wayne reminded me as the tickle machine did its work. "Three long hours this time."

"Ha, ha, ha, ha, ha, ha, ha, ha, ha, ha, ha, ha, ha, ha, ha!!!!!" I guffawed as my more than sensitive cock and balls were again being tickle tortured along with my poor sore nipples. "Ohhhhhh no, no, *y-you have got to be kidding me man!!!*"

My mouth grimaced into the shape of an "O" when I felt the rotating feathers burrowing into my wide sexy slit. My tied down wrists spasmed under the ropes and I felt myself getting harder than hard again.

"ohhhhhhh my poor cock," I muttered.

"Don't you mean your poor feet?" Wayne asked me, holding up the pen that had been on the small table.

"Oh God no, no, what now man?" I asked. "Ha, ha, ha, ha, ha, ha, ha, ha, ha, ha, ha!!!!!"

Wayne stepped to the foot of the table and I more than howled as he began writing my name on the bottom of one of my feet, followed by the words "Loves Linda."

"Harrrrrr, harrrrrrrrr, harrrrrrrrrr!!!!" I roared crazily as the feathers under the table tickled me and Wayne wrote on the bottoms of my feet my name and Linda's.

"Now you know why I had to have you so thoroughly restrained," Wayne said to me and moved his pen slowly over the bottom of my other foot. "Chris loves Linda…"

"Ha, ha, ha, ha, ha, ha, ha, ha, ha, ha, ha, ha, ha, ha, ha!!!!" was all I could say to that.

"Does Chris love Wayne as well?" my captor asked me and I felt the beginning of a "W" being written on my heel.

"Th-that's some line of shit!" I managed to say angrily as I felt Wayne's name being etched onto my heel. "HA, HA, HA, HA, HA, HA, HA!!!!!"

My restrained feet twitched uncontrollably as they were written on, the sharp tip of the pen tickling them horribly. I felt the words "Wayne loves Chris" being written onto my heel, just under where he had written my name and Linda's.

"F-fucker!!!!" I yelled laughingly. "HARRRRRRRR, ha, ha, ha, ha, ha, ha, ha, ha, ha, ha, ha!!!!!"

On my other heel I felt the words "Chris loves tickle torture" being written.

"OHHHHHHHHHRRRRR, ha, ha, ha, ha, ha, ha, ha, ha, ha!!!!!" was all I could say at that point.

Wayne then moved to the side of the table and wrote on the arches of my feet next. That really sent me soaring away in laughter let me tell you. I couldn't even concentrate hard enough to figure out the words he was etching onto my arches. I only knew that I was laughing uncontrollably at that point. The tips of the feathers tickling my cock had again burrowed themselves into my wide sexy slit. As they spun and spun in there my poor cock grew painfully hard…again. Obviously the aphrodisiac that Wayne had given me was still working its evil magic. Shooting my load earlier hadn't been enough to sate me it seemed.

When Wayne stopped writing on my feet my head seemed to spin away and all I heard after that was the sound of insane and lunatic laughter, my own insane and lunatic laughter. I could have sworn that at one point I shot another load under the table, GAWD, but I wasn't sure of anything though anymore. I also think that Wayne left me alone again for a while, while his evil feather machine did its notorious work on me. The next sound that I heard was Wayne's voice telling me that my three hours were up. The feather machine under the table was clicked off and I felt the restraints on my feet being undone.

"You did very well," I heard my captor's voice saying to me in a sort of echo sounding tone.

As he undid the restraints on my feet I laughed and cackled uncontrollably, even though I was no longer being tickled at that point.

"Hmmm, seems like I've caused you to become over sensitized my young handsome executive," Wayne said with a chuckle.

Fuck me softly buds, but every time he called me his young handsome executive my cock twitched. He then untied the ropes holding my cuffed wrists to the table and lifted me gently from the tabletop. I screamed with laughter as he hoisted me from under my arms and to my feet. Then, holding me by my upper arms with my head thrown back and my chest jutting out Wayne slowly walked me away from the table. My nipples had been torched up to the size of two bullets on my chest and I swear that if anyone had squeezed 'em at that moment I would have shot a load like crazy, I was that horny, that worked up. I was a sweaty and exhausted mess at that point and my cock was again hard as a fucking rock. God almighty, what had this fucker done to me? I glanced back at the zip lock bag that my socks were in and laughed stupidly, wondering how I was going to tell Linda that the socks she had given me had been stolen *and* right off my feet at that…

Again my head seemed to spin away and I passed out, fell into a super strong stupor is more like it…

"Ooops," I heard Wayne say in a caring tone as he caught me before

I hit the floor, caught me and scooped me up into his strong arms.

At that point the world went totally dark…

When I opened my eyes I was astonished and out rightly shocked to find myself of all places, back at the airport. I woke up in the seating area where passengers await their ride from the airport.

"Wh-what the hell?" I murmured, rubbing the sleep from my eyes as I woke up. "I-I'm at the airport…"

Looking around I saw two young girls sitting across from me. They looked to be in their mid twenties or so. They seemed to be drinking in the sight of me. I nervously reached for my tie and straightened it. My tie, *my tie???* Looking down quickly at myself I saw that I was wearing my suit. Relief like never before enveloped me. My suit hadn't been cut up like some old rag! It had all been a dream. As I realized that I smiled from ear to ear and the young girls sitting across from me really drank in the sight of me then. I got to my feet, saw my one piece of luggage at my feet and quickly picked it up, looking around for my ride, *my real ride…*

I walked away from the seating area looking for my usual driver who would be holding up the sign that read, "Chris's Ride." No doubt I hadn't seen him earlier and sat down to wait and fell asleep and had a bad fucking dream. As I was thinking this I saw an average built guy of about five feet nine inches tall holding up a sign that read, "Chris's Ride." He was nothing like Wayne from in my dream but he was my driver, my driver. I didn't know his name; only that he had picked me up from the airport numerous times and driven me home. I knew that I could trust him. I dashed over to him with my hand held out.

"Well now, there you are," he said to me with a smile. "I almost gave up on you young man."

"Glad you didn't," I said happily as he shook my hand. "I fell asleep in the seating area."

"Ah, long and boring business meeting I would guess," the forty to forty five year old driver said to me, almost the same thing that Wayne had said to me in my dream.

He let go of my hand as I looked at him nervously for a moment.

"Uh, where's the car?" I asked him. "I really am anxious to get home."

"Right this way," the driver said, leading the way to the main parking lot. "Would you like me to take your luggage for you?"

"No thanks, I'm fine," I replied as we approached a regal looking dark colored Cadillac.

I deposited my luggage in the trunk and sat down in the plush and comfortable back seat. The driver closed the door and climbed into the front seat.

"If you would care for a drink or something there's a full wet mini bar back there," the driver said, glancing at me in the rearview mirror. "Although from all the times you've been in my car I'm sure you know that already young man."

"Uh, no thanks," I said, looking at his eyes in the rearview mirror, then my mouth dropped open in total shock when I saw what was hanging from his mirror.

"H-holy fuck, my sheers, *my sheer socks!!!!*" I ranted when I saw them hanging from the rearview mirror.

I quickly looked down at my feet and saw that my socks weren't on them. I was wearing my shoes, but no socks!!! That was probably why those two girls inside the airport were smiling so slyly at me. They probably thought that I looked real silly and cute at the same time without any socks on my feet.

"H-how the hell did you get my damned socks?" I asked the driver angrily realizing that the suit I was wearing was one of the suits that had been in my luggage. "Oh shit, holy fucking shit; it wasn't a dream after all..."

I quickly reached for the door handle but to my horror saw no door handle. I was locked in...

"Shit, *let me out of here man*!!" I seethed, prepared to jump over into the front seat and exit the car that way if need be.

But it was at that moment that the clear partition was raised between the driver and me.

"What are you doing?" I ranted, clasping my fingers around the partition as it was raised, but it was controlled electronically and I couldn't hold it down.

I was forced to let go of it as it reached the top, lest my fingers get sliced off.

"*Shit!!! Shit!!!*" I screeched and flopped back in the back seat.

I quickly sat up and pounded on the thick plastic partition. The car started moving slowly.

"Where are you taking me man?" I roared, pounding on the partition with the palms of my trembling hands. "Oh GOD, ohhhhhhrrr fuck, I'm bein' kidnapped all over again!!"

I saw my driver press a button on his console and suddenly I smelled something real funny.

"Wh-what is that?" I gasped, trying to hold my breath as I felt myself suddenly getting woozy.

I fell back into the back seat of the car and looked out the window as we exited the airport parking lot. The two girls from inside the airport were looking at me adoringly...

"Ohhhhhh, my poor feet," I whispered, knowing what I was to be in for all over again.

Then, as the car headed for the highway I took one last look at my sheer socks hanging from the rearview mirror and the world went black...

The Boiler Room
Inspired by a Tickle Drawing by: Malex

"Uh, I don't think we're supposed to be down here bud," Sean, the new captain of the college football team said to me as we made our way down the steps to the musty, humid and warm boiler room.

"Trust me man, I do this all the time," I said to him reassuringly as the big six foot tall dark haired jock followed me slowly down the steps, toking and puffing the marijuana joint that he had purchased from me less than ten minutes ago. "The custodian is on his break and he always, *always* overstays it. I can't tell you how many times I've been down here to smoke a joint or two between classes. And even if I did get caught what the hell would he do anyway? The way he overstays his breaks he's got nothing on me."

"Yeah, that's all cool and good, but I'm here on a football scholarship that I won back in high school, the muscle jock said as we reached the bottom of the steps, taking a long and hearty toke of his joint. "AHHHHH, good stuff bud, real good fucking stuff. As I said, if *I* get caught doing this down here I could be thrown out of this college on my hard muscular butt."

"Relax dude, it ain't going to happen," I said to him reassuringly and gave one of his wide and broad shoulders a squeeze as he looked around the dimly lit boiler room. "And I'm glad you like the stuff I sell. Like my buddy that sent you to me said, I get the best stuff that money can buy."

The football jock took another hard toke, held it in and then let it out slowly.

"Fuuuuccckkk, that is for sure bud," he said breathlessly, quickly taking yet another toke.

"Hey, take it slow muscle boy," I said to him, taking him by his upper muscular biceps. "I have plenty more stuff on me, and you know that because you're a first time customer I'm not going to charge you for the extras. Come on, let me show you around down here, show you how relaxing it is and why it's the perfect place to come to get a little high between classes."

"Right you are bud," the jock said with a grin as I held his upper arm and walked him deeper into the boiler room.

His name was Sean Curtis. He was twenty years old with looks that went beyond the words gorgeous or handsome. He could have graced the front cover page of GQ magazine without a problem he had movie star looks. He had dark hair, cut short and parted at the side, sort of like a banker. I guessed that his daddy was a banker or a broker or something corporate like that. His eyes were chestnut brown, deep and seductive. Fuck, I supposed that he knew that when it came to women he could have his pick of the litter, although he didn't seem to be overly conceited or narcissistic about his looks. He was six feet tall give or take an inch and was totally lean and muscular from the daily workouts that he obviously put himself through on a daily basis. It was September the beginning of the new semester and it was Sean Curtis' third week at the college. He had come to the elite college on a football scholarship that he had won for being his high school's star player. He had been the captain of his high school's football team and now he would be the captain of the college's team. Sure as shit that Sean Curtis was on his way to the big leagues. He knew that he had to keep his grades in his required classes up there as well, if he wanted to stay in the elite college. If not then the big muscle boy would be thrown right out on what he had called his hard muscular butt. Both of us dressed in knee length shorts, over-sized tee shirts and sneakers with white sweat socks we made our way deeper into the underground boiler room, the smell of marijuana wafting around us as the football jock lit his second joint.

"MMMMM, awesome," he said, standing there towering over me as he took a hearty toke. "Fucking A man, totally fucking A!"

The only problem that Sean Curtis had was his obvious need to get high. He claimed that it assisted him in staying awake, concentrating on his studies and he said that it even helped him in his football game. I knew for a fact that the handsome executive's son was full of shit. He was a marijuana addict, plain and simple. When he had learned of my services at the college he searched me out like a cat after catnip. When I first set eyes on him I thought he had to be the handsomest thing I had ever seen in my life. I also thought of the boiler room and the device that I kept hidden down there for what I call my "extra special customers."

"Man, it's fucking hot down here bud," the jock said, handed me his joint to hold for a second and shucked off his tee shirt, revealing a wide muscular smooth chest, a hard six pack stomach, thick bowling ball like biceps ripped triceps and shoulders as wide as a doorway. He dangled his tee shirt out of the back pocket of his shorts and quickly took the joint back from me, sticking it between his pursed lips and sucking on it with utter gusto. Two very fleshy and eraser head-like nipples adored the big muscle boy's smooth chest. They looked real meaty and the tips of them were overly pointy, as if calling out for some much-needed attention.

"Colombian?" he asked me, holding up the joint in front of me.

"Sure as shit," I replied with a grin as we headed for some wooden stacked crates.

"Fuck man, if I were a faggot I would kiss you," he said with a chuckle. "Believe you me bud, you got a permanent customer here."

"Glad to hear that," I said and pointed out the crates, wallowing in the sight of the two big pink fleshy nipples that adorned his massive chest. "Come on, let's sit down and take a load off…"

"As my exec dad would say, sounds like a plan," the football jock said and lowered himself onto a wooden crate, leaning his wide back against the two pipes behind him.

I sat down on a crate diagonally next to him and took a third joint out of my pocket. He looked at it longingly, but then his eyes focused with curiosity on the strange looking device that was standing a few feet in front of the crate he was seated on.

"Say bud, what's that thing?" Sean Curtis asked me, looking at the device with more than curiosity as he took a hearty toke on what was left of his second joint.

"It's a relaxation device," I said, glancing at the thing, trying to sound as if I was not interested.

So far my plan was working like a charm, as usual, get the jock seated close enough to the thing for it to catch his eye and then hope that he asks about it. The device was actually two square pieces of wood mounted on a heavy-duty plastic platform. The top half of the wood swung back and forth and locked into the lower half. In the center of the wooden structure were two round holes, big enough for a jock like Sean Curtis to slide his size twelve feet comfortably into.

"A relaxation device?" the jock asked. "What the hell kind of relaxation device is that? And if that's so what the hell is it doing down here in the boiler room?"

"I think the custodian uses it," I explained. "Although he's really not supposed to."

"Fuck, but this custodian should be fired bud," Sean laughed, dropping the tail end of his joint on the floor. "He overstays his breaks and he uses stuff that he's not supposed to. Shit!!"

"Yeah, he really should be canned," I said agreeably.

I felt awful badmouthing the custodian but it sure was helping where my plan was concerned.

"Just how does that thing work as a relaxation device?" the jock asked me, the question that I was praying he would ask me.

"Well, the way I think it works is that you slip your feet into these two holes here," I said, pointing at the two holes on the structure. "And then you just sit back and stretch your legs out as far as possible."

"Is that it?" he asked me, taking the third joint from me and tucking it up behind his ear, obviously planning to save it for use later on.

I could tell from his watery eyes that he was on a real good high at that point...

"Man, the way I'm feeling now I sure could use some good ol' relaxation," the big jock said and lifted his big feet. "Open the top of that thing for me would you bud? The way I'm feeling from the good stuff I just smoked I can let my head spin a little while I'm relaxin' here."

"Sure thing," I said, not believing my luck where this little adventure was concerned.

"Yeah, get my big ol' feet in that relaxation thing and just let my head spin," the jock crooned with his feet hefted and his eyes all glazed over.

I opened the top portion of the device and Sean Curtis lowered his big feet into it. Without a word I slowly closed the top of the device, latching it shut at the side. Now all I had to do was get the guy's arms restrained to the pipes behind him. For that I would have to be faster than fast and his being so high and wrecked at the moment helped me immensely...

"Man, I don't feel relaxed at all, if anything I feel silly," the big jock said. "I mean, look at that shit, my big ol' size twelve's in there."

Smiling wickedly he jiggled his sneakered feet a few times...

"Well, it helps if you lean back against the pipes behind you," I said, stepping next to him and pressing one of his broad shoulders back. "And then really stretching your legs out as far as possible."

"Okay, I'll give that a shot," the smooth muscle boy said, pressing his arms against the pipes.

Standing beside him at that point I slowly and with my hands shaking took a goodly length of rope out of the left side pocket of my shorts. Fuck, if I were going to do this I would have to be faster than fast. He was a football jock after all and I was sure he had good reflexes.

"Yeah, that helps a little bud," he said, leaning back with his arms pressed one each against the pipes. "Damn, check it out though bud, with the top of that thing locked down on the device my feet are actually trapped in there."

As he said that and tried to lift his feet up to push the top of the device open I squatted beside him, right where his wrists were pressed against the pipe behind him. I licked my lips and in a fast move wound the rope around the pipes and quickly pulled it tightly around the jock's wrists, pinning them to the pipes.

"H-hey, what're you doin' bud?" he asked me, suddenly sounding very nervous. "Is tyin' me to the pipes part of the relaxation technique?"

"Yeah, you might say that," I snickered meanly and made sure that the ropes around his wrists were tighter than tight.

When I was done tying his wrists to the pipes I took another length of rope from my right side pocket. I quickly tied his forearms to the pipes as well.

"H-hey man, I'm startin' to think that there's some funny business going on here," Sean Curtis said in his marijuana haze. "I'm startin' to think I've been had somehow…"

"Well, it is going to be funny Sean that I can assure you of," I said reassuringly, as I took a long length of rope out of my back pocket and stood up straight. "It's going to be so funny that you're going to be laughing your big muscle head off."

Looking up at me the big shirtless jock watched as I wound the long length of rope under his massive male cleavage, looped it over and around his shoulders and yanked it tight, pinning him to the pipes at that point.

"Wh-what're you doin' man?" he asked miserably, trying unsuccessfully to get his hands free. "What's the point of this?"

Once I had him tied securely I stepped to his feet in the device and squatted down near them…

"Comfortable?" I asked him and gingerly ran a hand over the top of one of his sneakers.

"I don't know man," he replied. "I got to admit I'm a little confused here."

"Hmmm, maybe you should smoke another joint," I suggested.

"No, the one behind my ear is for later bud," the jock said.

"This one will be a bonus," I said, taking a fatter than usual joint from my tee shirt pocket, the one I had been saving for when I got the muscle boy all tied up.

I stretched across, placed the joint between his lips and lit it for him. Then I returned my attention to his big trapped feet.

"Go ahead bud, suck and toke on that for a while," I said to him, starting to unlace his sneakers.

"When are you going to untie me man?" he asked through pursed lips, toking hard on the joint, holding the smoke in and then letting it out the sides of his mouth. "Ohhhh man, this is strong stuff you got me smoking here."

"Oh, not for a while Curtis, not for a long while," I said with a grin and slid his left sided sneaker off his big size twelve foot.

"H-hey man, what're you up to now?" he asked as the smoke was irritating his eyes as it wafted up. "Taking my sneakers off me? Fuck man, not a good idea, seeing as I have the stinkiest socks in the whole fucking world."

Just what I was hoping for actually...

"But if you want to massage my stinky socked feet while they're in that gizmo it's your funeral bud," the jock snickered around the joint in his mouth.

As he puffed and toked hard on the joint some ashes fell off it and landed all over his massive chest.

"Oh man, I'm makin' a mess here bud," the muscle jock said. "Better untie me from this relaxation device, or whatever the fuck it is that you call it."

But instead I untied the laces on his right sneaker and slid that one off him next. The scent of the jock's socks wafted up and assaulted my nostrils. I couldn't resist stealing a few good hearty sniffs of the insides of his big sneakers.

He was right his sneakers were laced with the scent of his stinky sweat socks, total heaven to say the least.

"Ohhhhh man, don't be doin' that man," the jock said and puffed hard again on the fat joint, more ashes tumbling from his lips and landing on his massive chest. "Either I'm seeing things because I'm so high here or you're sniffin' the insides of my raunchy sneakers. Heh!!! Total stinking foot jam I bet bud!!!"

He leaned his head back, pursed his lips tight around the fat joint and with his eyes squeezed shut in a sort of ecstasy he inhaled deep...

"MMMMM, fucking massive smoke bud," the football jock crooned, held the smoke in a few seconds and then let it out slowly. "This shit is better than the other stuff you gave me before."

Slowly, he lowered his head and looked to see me squatting there with my hands pressed tightly around the centers of his trapped feet. I was squeezing and massaging them as the smell of his musty and moist white sweat socks wafted up at me...

"Hmmmm, have to admit that feels nice bud," Sean Curtis snickered. "But I don't want you perving all over my feet, know what I mean? I'll let you massage 'em for me and all, seeing as you got me hooked up to your relaxation gizmo here, but no pervin'."

He snickered and then puffed at the joint again…

"Fucking fuck man, wh-what's in this thing?" he asked as he let the smoke out the sides of his mouth. "I'm startin' to feel kind of, shit, hate to have to admit man, but I'm feelin' real randy and horny here all of a sudden…"

Also just what I was hoping for…

"Well, that joint you're presently smoking has some vitamin and herb powders mixed in it," I explained to the jock as I began working at getting his socks off him, peeling them slowly off his smelly feet. "It's also laced with some potent minerals from the orient. So besides the marijuana in it you're also smoking an aphrodisiac of sorts…"

"A-aphrodisiac?" he stammered at me and held what was left of the joint between his lips, watching in wonderment as I peeled his socks off him.

"*Wh-what are you doin' bud?*" he asked, starting to realize what I was up to at that point. "First my sneakers and now my damned smelly socks? What is this shit? *You got a thing for my feet or something?*"

"You could say that," I mused and leaned down to sniff his toes a few times.

"Fuck man, *holy shit, untie me you freak,*" he snarled, the joint stuck to his lower lip, no longer lit at that point. "FUCK, fucking guy, sniffing my stinking toes!! Shit, girls I've dated and taken to the bedroom have complained that my feet smelled so bad that they wouldn't go near 'em. And now look at you man, *fucking sniffing at my sneakers, takin' my sweaty socks off me and now sniffing my damned cheesy toes of all things!*"

He struggled mightily but to no avail as I sadled up next to him. I produced my lighter and held it to the joint.

"Smoke bud, smoke," I whispered in his ear, my lips grazing his lobe. "Smoke this stuff, you're about to go flying like never before in your life…"

As I held the small joint between his lips he reluctantly puffed and toked it, looking at me angrily from the corner of his eye…

"F-fucker," he whispered angrily and I saw the tent that his cock had made in his shorts. "Y-you tricked me into all this shit bud. Gods, I'm flying higher than a kite…"

I smiled triumphantly. I was almost ready…

I held the tiny piece that was left of the joint to the jock's pursed lips as he smoked what was left of it, puffing it hard, not wanting to admit that he needed the stuff desperately. When he was done I dropped the tiny piece of rolled paper on the floor and brushed the stray ashes off his magnificent chest, giving his delectable nipple tips a few good squeezes.

"Arrrrhhhh man, d-don't be squeezin' and teasin' my man tits bud," the muscle boy crooned, his head lolling around and against the pipes. "Th-that shit always bones me the fuck up like you can't believe."

"Oh I can believe it Curtis," I said laughingly, looking at the now massive bulge in his shorts.

When his chest was cleaned of the ashes I stepped back over to his trapped feet. He watched as I picked up one of his sweat socks and pressed it hard against my nose and mouth, inhaling his stinky foot odor with utter gusto, even licking his rancid sock a few times.

"Come on man, untie me already," Sean Curtis grunted in his haze. "Shit, all this just so you could sniff and taste my smelly socks?"

I put his sock down next to his sneakers and other sock and then reached into one of the stacked crates and brought out what I call my bag of tricks, actually a large backpack filled with my nasty surprises. Now I was readier than ready...

"Wh-what's with the bag bud?" he asked me nervously, watching as I took out a battery powered toothbrush.

"I call this my bag of tricks muscle boy," I said to the bound jock and clicked on the toothbrush.

The thing came to high powered life in my hand, buzzing like crazy, the sound filling the air around us, the bristles vibrating at what looked like a hundred miles per hour.

I smiled fiendishly as I brought the vibrating bristles closer and closer to the jock's trapped bare feet.

"Oh no, no, *oh fuck man*, you wouldn't," Sean Curtis grunted, struggling more than ever now to pull free of the binding ropes.

"Are you ticklish Sean?" I asked him, holding the toothbrush less than a few mere inches away from the bottom of one of his feet.

"Y-yeah man, I-I'm real ticklish," he whimpered in his drugged haze.

"Just what I wanted to hear," I said and pressed the vibrating bristles hard against the beefy bottom of his right foot, swirling the brush around and around.

"Oh no, *no*, ha, ha, ha, ha, ha, ha, ha, ha, ha, ha, ha, ha, ha!!!!!" the jock laughed loudly all of a sudden, bucking under the tight ropes.

"Also just what I wanted to hear," I chuckled and swirled the vibrating bristles more and more over the bottom of his right foot, moving down to his beefy heel and back up again.

"Y-you fucker, you pervert," the football jock laughed. "Har, har, har, har, har, ohhhhrrrr fuck, ha, ha, ha, ha, ha, I-I'm bein' tickle tortured here!!! GAWWWWWD, of all the fucked up things!!"

Holding the toothbrush against the bottom of his right foot I slid my fingertips over the bottom of his left foot, tickling that one as well now.

"Ohhhhhhhhhh ha, ha, ha, ha, ha, ha, ha, ha, ha, ha, ha!!!!" Sean Curtis roared, his head thrown back, as I tickled both his feet now.

"So glad you searched me out you big muscle head," I said gleefully and switched feet, tickling his left foot now with the vibrating toothbrush and his right foot with my fingertips.

"Ha, ha, ha, ha, ha, ha, ha, ha, ha, ha, ha!!!" the bound football jock laughed, his massive chest cleavage jiggling under the binding ropes.

I noticed that the tent in his shorts had become more pronounced as I tickled him...

"L-let me go bud, turn me loose, ha, ha, ha, ha, ha, ha, ha, ha, ha, ha!!!" the jock laughed and gasped.

I alternated with the toothbrush on the bottoms of his feet, along his arches, over his heels and just under his sexy toes. Whenever I was working one of his beefy feet with the toothbrush I made sure to be finger tickling his other foot at the same time. I didn't want either of his feet to feel left out after all...

"Harrrrhhh, harrrr, har, ha, ha, ha, ha, ha, ha, ha, ha!!!!" the jock laughed and laughed, starting to sweat after a while.

"Ha, ha, ha, ha, ha, ha, ha, ha, ohhhhhrrrr man, you fuck head," Sean Curtis sputtered. "S-see if I'll be a customer to you after this shit!!! Ha, ha, ha, ha, ha, ha, ha, ha, ha, ha, ha, ha!!!!"

"Oh you'll still be my customer muscle boy," I said and pressed the toothbrush against his foot, hard. "And not only will you continue buying marijuana from me, but you'll be back for more of this as well."

"W-we'll see about that man, ha, ha, ha, ha, ha, ha, ha, ha, ha, ohhhhrrrrr SHHHIITT," the football player spat.

With an intent look on my face I swirled the toothbrush over his feet alternately as fast as possible sending chills and thrills of tickle torture through my bound up jock boy.

"Harrrrrr, harrr, harrrr, ha, ha, ha, ha, ha, ha!!!!" Sean Curtis' laughter echoed loudly through the boiler room.

After a good twenty to twenty five minutes of tickle torture with the battery powered toothbrush I turned it off and placed it on the floor next to the jock's sneakers and socks.

"Th-thank you man, oh shit, that, *that was awful*," the jock said, catching his breath. "Guess you do that to all your first time customers eh bud? Your way of initiating them huh?"

"You could say that Sean," I said snidely, making sure that he was breathing normally.

I watched as his big sweaty chest heaved up and down, his big nipples even more prominent and sensitive looking now, the tips of them all erect and jutted up.

"Well, I for one am glad that's over with," the jock said. "Now if you would untie me so I can be on my way…"

"Over? Untie you?" I asked him, sounding surprised as I reached into my bag of tricks again. "Muscle boy, I'm just getting started on you here. Classes for you are canceled for today."

As I spoke he looked at me in utter horror and then his eyes opened wider when he saw the next items I took from my bag of tricks, a few toothpicks.

"H-hey, c'mon now man, you can't keep me down here," he began and then his words were cut short when I slid two of the toothpicks between the toes of both his feet.

"Ohhhhhrrr shit, n-not my toes you fucker!!" the jock boy railed, trying most unsuccessfully to stifle his laughter as I slid the toothpicks back and forth between his toes on both his feet at the same time. "Ha, ha, ha, ha, ha, ha, ha, ha, ha, ha, ha, ha, ha, ha, ha, ha, ohhhhhhhhh f-fuck, I-I'm goin' to report this horseplay to the dean fuck head!!"

"Yeah?" I asked him meanly and slid the tips of the toothpicks over the balls of his feet, just under his wriggling toes and then back between his toes again. "And what will you tell the dean Curtis? That you were smoking marijuana in the boiler room and that a drug dealer managed to convince you to place your big old feet in a tickle trap?"

"Ohhhhrrrrr GAWD, ha, ha, ha, ha, ha, ha, ha, ha, ha, ha, ha!!!!!" the jock laughed, his massive chest and male cleavage bouncing up and down erotically under the ropes, his cock stand harder than hard at that point in his shorts.

He was obviously coming to realize the fruitlessness of telling the dean or anyone else at the college about this little adventure that I'd tricked him into...

I slid the toothpicks between each of his toes at a fast pace on both his feet and each time I moved them he laughed louder and louder and louder...

Like with the toothbrush before them I tickled Sean Curtis with the toothpicks for a good twenty to twenty five minutes or so...

When I stopped tickling him with the toothpicks I looked hungrily at the bulge in his shorts. The muscle boy was gasping for breath, sweating, his head hanging down. I figured I had better give him something to drink. I didn't want him dehydrating and passing out on me after all. I was only having some mean fun with him I didn't need to be rushing him to the college infirmary.

"Thirsty Curtis?" I asked the muscle boy.

"Y-yeah, yeah, g-guess I am at that," the jock said, looking up at me with glazed eyes, his laughter still showing in them. "B-being tickle tortured really racks a guy, as I'm finding out here bud..."

"Yeah, and I'm going to make sure you keep finding out Muscle head," I murmured. "Now, let's get you something hearty to drink."

Smiling meanly I took a bottle of warm mineral water from a crate and held it to the jock's lips, my other hand under his chin.

"Down the hatch Curtis," I said softly and watched intently as his lips sucked at the mouth of the bottle. He

stopped for breath in between long gulps and by the time he was done half the quart-sized bottle of water was gone.

AHHHHH, thanks man, guess I was really thirsty at that huh?" he asked me with his head leaned back against the pipes and his eyes half closed in a sort of ecstasy.

I was guessing that the aphrodisiac he had smoked really was having an effect on him at that point…

I put the bottle down and unable to help myself leaned down slowly toward the jock's half-opened mouth and his pouting lips. When I pressed my lips against his he briefly opened his eyes wide in shock, but when I kissed him I found him responding to me.

"F-fucker, you just kissed me man," Sean Curtis said angrily when I reluctantly pried my lips away from his. "Listen man, I'm no faggot…"

"No muscle head?" I asked him meanly, reaching for the zipper on his shorts. "We're going to find out about that, *and right now…*"

In a quick move I yanked his zipper down…

"H-hey, wh-what the fuck are you up to now man???" the jock bellowed, watching with his eyes open wide in disbelief as I reached into the wide fly opening of his shorts.

He was totally breathless as I unceremoniously brought his big beefy jock cock and his plum-sized hairless sweaty balls out of his shorts. His cock and balls smelled as gummy and randy as his big feet.

"HUUUUHHHH fuck, *bastard*, inspecting my big meat pole," the muscle boy gasped as I held his better than seven inches tightly in my fist. "Fuck man, I'm goin' to get you for this shit bud!!"

Chuckling, I let go of his cock and then he was even more breathless. I guessed that having his meat stick held and handled was better than not. I picked up the electric toothbrush and switched it on to high speed. Once again the sounds of the thing whirring to life filled the air in the musty boiler room and the bristles vibrated at nearly a hundred miles per hour. I looked at the toothbrush with sinister eyes and an evil grin on my face, the way a villain might have done in those old movies where he had captured the super-hero.

"Wh-what're you up to now pervert?" the tied up muscle jock babbled fearfully, watching as I moved my hand with the whirring toothbrush in it closer and closer to his hard cock. "*Oh no, no, not that you sick fuck!!! Ohhhhhrrrrrrr shiiiiiitttttt, ha, ha, ha, ha, ha, ha, ha, ha, ha, ha, ha, ha, ha!!!!!!! Ohhhh GAAAWWDDDD!!!*"

He more than heaved and struggled under the tight ropes, sweating like crazy, laughing uncontrollably as I slid the whirling bristles of the toothbrush over and over and around and around the shaft of his hard cock.

"Harrrrrr, harrrrrrhhhh, ha, ha, ha, ha, ha, ha, ha, ha, ha, ha!!!!!" the jock laughed loudly, his voice echoing and bouncing off the walls of the boiler room. "T-ticklin' my damned cock!!! Ha, ha, ha, ha, ha, ha, ha, ha, ha, ha, ha!!!! N-never heard of such madness!!!! Harrrrrhhhh harrrrr ha, ha, ha, ha, ha, ha!!!!"

As I trailed the toothbrush all over his shaft his cock twitched and jiggled between his legs, pearly droplets of pre cum and beads of piss forming on his wide sexy slit. I grinned at that. I moved the toothbrush down over his balls and he cackled louder still as I massaged and tickled his low hangers.

"Haaaaaaaahhhhhhhh, n-not my big ol' nuts too you bastard!!!!" he screamed. "F-fuck it all, *this is a shitty thing to be doin' to the captain of the college football team bud!!!! Ha, ha, ha, ha, ha, ha, ha, ha, ha, ha, ha, ohhhhrrr man, y-you're roastin' my nuts with that toothbrush bud!!!'*

I watched as still more droplets of pre cum and piss beaded up on his wide piss slit. His slit bobbed open and closed like a third eye and its sticky fluid slid down the sides of his shaft. With that evil looking grin back on my face I moved the toothbrush up toward his pre cumming slit.

"Ohhhhhh, wh-what now???" he gasped, watching as I slid the whirling bristles up the length of his big shaft. Ha, ha, ha, ha, ha, ha, ha, ha, ha, ha, ha, ha, ha, ha, ha, ha, ha, ha!!!!!!"

When I got to the crown of his cock I held the whirling bristles against his slit. That sent him into a frenzy the likes of which I had never seen before.

"AYYYYYYYYYRRRRRRRR!!!!! Ha, ha, ha, ha, ha, ha, ha, ha, ha, ha, ha, ha!!!!!" he guffawed crazily. "Oh fucking fuck, not my slit you pervert!!!!"

I caressed the tip of his slit with the bristles and more and more of his good stuff oozed from it.

"Fuck it all Curtis, this cock of yours hasn't gone down once since I started working you over," I commented and grabbed his shaft with my other hand as I tickle tortured and tickle tortured and tickle tortured his piss slit.

With a maniacal looking smile on my face I swirled that toothbrush around and around and around his slit, stroking his hard cock every fifteen seconds or so.

"F-fucking pervert, sick bastard, jackin' me off and ticklin' me," he gasped incoherently. "Harrrrrhhhh, ha, ha, ha, ha, ha, ha, ha, ha, ha, ha, ha!!!!!"

With his lips pursed at one point and spittle flying from the sides of his mouth I thought for sure he was going to beg me to stroke his cock, as I had stopped doing that and was just tickling his slit.

"PPPPPHHHHFFFFFF!!!!! Ha, ha, ha, ha, ha, ha, ha, ha, ha, haaaaaaaaa!!!!!" the muscle boy shrieked loudly then. "*Ohhhhhrrrr g-god bud, I-I don't believe what the fuck is about to happen here!!!!*"

As he blurted his words I felt his cock more than twitching as I simply held it in my hand. I quickly moved the toothbrush off his slit. Both of us watched in amazement as Sean Curtis' cock spewed forth a hearty and abundant load of football player juices.

"Ohhhhhrrrrrr f-fuck, lookit this shit, got me creaming like a damned bitch in heat bud!!!!" the muscled jock crowed in a mixture of ecstasy and anger as his mess landed and splattered all over his massive chest, his pecs, his nipples and dripped down to his stomach region.

I held his cock tight in my fist and he shuddered and was all sweaty in the tight bondage as he spewed more mess.

"HUUUUHHHHHRRR FUCK," he grunted throatily as I squeezed every possible drop of his mess from him.

He sat there panting and gasping for breath, his big smelly feet twitching in the tickle torture device, his big toes wiggling.

"G-goin' to get you for this man," Sean Curtis whimpered miserably. "See if I'm kiddin' you."

"Looks like that aphrodisiac I made you smoke really made you more than potent Muscle head," I said to him, still holding tight to his pulsing and semi hardness. "Let's see what this does…"

That said I turned the electric toothbrush back on and again swirled it over his slit.

"OHHHHrrrrrrr no, oh *jeez Louise man, st-stop tickle torturin' my damned muscle pipe!!!*" he pleaded as I stroked him a few times. "An-and st-stop strokin' me man, after I shoot a load I'm all sensitive and sexy down there!!! Ha, ha, ha, ha, ha, ha, ha, ha, ha, ha, ha, ha, f-fucker, y-you ain't listenin' to me bud!!"

"Oh I'm listening," I said snidely. "And I totally agree you're real sexy down here!"

With that I turned off the electric toothbrush and stroked the jock's cock a few times. To his total shock he spewed forth a second load of his frothy jock boy juices.

"AYYYYYYYRRRR shiiiiitttt, n-never came again so soon bud," he garbled as his second mess added to the one already all over his massive torso.

He bucked and writhed in the tight bondage as I stroked and stroked his thick creamy sperm from him…

"AHHHHHHHHHH!!!!" he garbled loudly as the last of his mess spurted from his cock. "I-I'm feelin' crazy here you perv…"

He leaned his head back against the pipes he was bound to, his hair all sweaty and now slicked to his head. He breathed heavily and loudly as I put the electric toothbrush in my backpack, a look of slight relief filling his face…that is, until I took out the two long sharp-tipped feathers.

"Oh no man," he whimpered, almost crying at that point.

His cock went semi soft and large beads of piss emanated from it and trickled down the sides of his shaft. I wondered how long he would be able to hold out while being tickle tortured some more…

"Ha, ha, ha, ha, ha, ha, ha, ha, ha, ha, ha, ha, ha!!!!" was the sound filling the boiler room all over again as I now stood over the jock's stretched out legs, my legs parted around them.

I leaned down and tickle tortured the hard tips of his nipples with the feather tips.

"Ohhhhhhrrrr sh-sh-SHIT, l-leave my man tits alone you sick fuck!!!" he screamed up at me. "Ha, ha, ha, ha, ha, ha, ha, ha, ha, ha, ha, ha, ha, ha!!!! Af-after shooting a load my man tits are as sexy and sensitive as my muscle pipe you bastard!!! Ha, ha, ha, ha, ha, ha, ha, ha, ha, an-and fuck it all, I just shot two, ha, ha, ha, ha, ha, ha, ha, two damned loads, so my man tits are doubly sensitive right now. HARRRRRRhhhhh, ha, ha, ha, ha, ha, ha, ha, ha!!!!"

"Exactly what I was counting on Curtis," I chuckled and twirled the feather tips against the tips of what he called his man tits.

With his head pressed hard against the pipes and his hair all sweaty and dripping the jock boy laughed and laughed as I tickle tortured his nipples. He screamed his laughter when I moved one of the feather tips into his piss trickling slit while still tickling one of his nipples.

"OOOOOHHHHHH ha, ha, ha, ha, ha, ha, ha, ha, ha, ha, ha, ha, ha!!!!" he chortled helplessly. "Y-you're goin' to make me crazy here bud, ha, ha, ha, ha, ha, ha, ha, ha!!!!"

"Oh I think you're stronger than that Curtis," I said snidely and alternated tickling his nipples at the same time and tickling his piss slit and a nipple at the same time.

Watching me his eyes darted up and down and then finally he whimpered, "I got to f-fucking piss," between his bouts of uncontrollable laughter. Just what I was waiting to hear I thought fiendishly. At his words of needing to piss I stopped tickling him (just temporarily) and picked up the empty mineral water bottle.

"Okay Curtis, piss till your heart's content," I said merrily, inserting his piss slit into the mouth of the water bottle, holding his shaft good and tight.

"I-I can't piss on command like that bud, I'm what they call pee shy," he grunted miserably.

I shrugged, gave his cock a few tugs and then a second or two later he was pissing liberally and frothily into the bottle.

"AHHHHHHHH oh yeah, yeah, s-seems like you've taken control of my knob, n-never felt so damned good to piss bud," he sputtered as he pissed and pissed and pissed into the bottle.

When he was done he could not believe the amount that he had pissed into the bottle...

While he sat there catching his breath and sweating like a pig I took a moment to step to the side and piss into the bottle as well, mixing my mess with his while standing over him at the same time.

"Enjoying your time in the relaxation device Curtis?" I asked him as I relieved myself into the bottle.

"Y-you fucker, wh-when are you plannin' on letting me out of here?" he asked me. "I've already missed a couple of my classes already

I'm sure."

"I told you, classes for you are canceled today," I replied, finished pissing.

I capped the bottle and put it down next to my backpack of tricks for use later on...

"All you have to do today is get high, get horny and get tickled," I said meanly, taking another fat joint from my pocket.

The jock simply looked at me blankly as I slipped the joint between his lips and lit it for him. Without me having to tell him what to do so he started toking and puffing heartily on it.

"Errrrrhhhh shit, th-this is another of those Spanish flies you got me smokin' here bud," he sniveled through his lips as he puffed and inhaled. "I can feel it in my cock already..."

Smiling meanly I made sure he really smoked and puffed the joint... No cheating for my latest tickle victim...

When he was done with the joint I took the tiny end of it from between his lips and dropped it on the floor. Squatting beside him I looked sideways into his more than glazed eyes, twisting and tweaking one of his nipples at the same time...

"Y-you fucker," he whispered. "Turn me loose already...god, feels like I'm on clouds nine and ten and eleven bud..."

I snickered knowingly, let go of his nipple, noted how hard his cock was again and blindfolded him for the next round of tickle torture...

"We have a lot more to do down here before I turn you loose Curtis," I said to him, knotting the white cloth blindfold behind his head.

"F-fuck man, what now, blindfolding me???" he asked miserably. "Shit man, this is getting scary now bud."

Once he was plunged totally into darkness I took the scalp massager out of my backpack. It's a round device that is held by a handle on one side and on the other side it has what looks like a thousand or so round rivulets on it, rivulets that spin at an intensely high speed all at the same time. Used on a bald scalp it can be very soothing. Used on tickle sensitive areas of the body it can be out-right torture. Holding the device by the handle I clicked it on. The rotary sound of the rivulets spinning and coming to life filled the room and my bound up jock boy looked around stupidly with his blindfolded eyes...

"Wh-what's that sound bud?" he asked me as I moved the scalp massager toward his six pack stomach area. "Wh-what is that???"

But then, the only sounds he was able to make were that of raucous laughter, literally a belly laugh this time around. I pressed the scalp massager against his six pack abs and he couldn't even form words anymore.

"ARRRRRHHHHHHH, ha, ha, ha, ha, ha, ha, ha, ha, ha, ha, ha, ha, ha, ha, ha, ha, ha!!!!!" he sputtered and cackled as the high speed spinning rivulets rubbed meanly against his stomach region.

"Good thing I blindfolded you for this round eh Curtis?" I asked him snidely.

"HARRRRRR, harrrrrr, ha, ha, ha, ha, ha, ha, ha, ha, ha!!!!" was his reply, his blindfold sticking to his sweaty face. "HA, HA, HA, HA, HA, HA, HA, HA, HA, HA, HARRRRRHHHHHH!!!!"

I slowly rubbed the scalp massager against his stomach, swirling it around and around as I went. His cock throbbed big and hard between his legs and from the way he was laughing I am sure that he thought he was going to lose his mind…

After a good half-hour of tickle torturing his stomach region with the scalp massager I took the blindfold off him and moved back down to his trapped feet with the scalp massager.

"OHHHHH no, no," he stammered, able to speak for but a moment while not being tickled while I switched positions.

When I pressed the scalp massager against the bottoms of his feet alternately he was again laughing to the point where he could not form words.

"Your laughter is like music to my ears Curtis," I murmured. "If the guys on your football team could see their captain now…"

I tickled his sweaty and smelly feet for a good fifteen minutes with the scalp massager and then clicked it off. The well-muscled jock sat there gasping and stinking in his sweat.

"Wh-where's that damned custodian?" he garbled somewhat incoherently. "Wh-why hasn't he returned from his break?"

"Oh, didn't I tell you?" I asked the football jock snidely. "Today is his day off…"

This time it was my turn to laugh as a look of total wretchedness filled the muscle boy's handsome face and he leaned his head back against the pipes again. He sat there catching his breath slowly.

"I-I'm so thirsty again bud, how about more of that mineral water?" he asked me, sounding more like he was pleading.

"Hmmm, sorry to disappoint you Curtis, but we're all out of mineral water," I said, picking up the bottle of our combined piss. "This was the only bottle I brought with me. I didn't think you would finish the whole thing in one gulping. Then again, I didn't think you were going to fall for my little tickle torture game down here."

"Fuck man, *I'm thirsty,*" he ranted. "With all that you're doing to me here the least you can do is get me something to fucking drink…"

But then, he realized his mistake at what he had just said as I slowly uncapped the bottle of piss…

"Oh no, y-you wouldn't," Sean Curtis garbled more than angrily as I squatted down next to him and held the bottle of piss under his trembling lips. *"Pl-please man…"*

"If I were you I would drink it down Curtis," I said to him. "I plan to tickle torture you for quite a while more bud. And just look at that hard on you got from the aphrodisiac you just smoked. More than likely I'll get a good load or two more out of you as well."

He blinked his glazed eyes a few times, said, "Shitty ass thing to be doing to a guy," and puckered his lips as I slid the bottle between them. With a look of abhorrence etched on his handsome chiseled face he guzzled down the piss as quickly as possible.

"There you go Curtis, down the hatch," I said mockingly.

He didn't waste a single drop. The college football star guzzled down every drop of his and my rancid piss. When he was done he licked his lips a few times, hacked and coughed and looked at me with a look that if looks could kill I would have been dead…

Well, never one to waste time I quickly got back to the task at hand…

I reached into my backpack (my bag of tricks) and brought out two long thin bristled paint brushes…

This time Sean Curtis simply gulped hard…

"Ha, ha, ha, ha, ha, ha, ha, ha, ha, ha, ha, ha!!!!" the muscled jock laughed a few moments later as I squatted down in front of his trapped feet, running the paint brush bristles up and down the bottoms, balls, heels and toes of his feet. "Wh-what a twisted turn of events this is bud!!! N-never thought that some dude would want to t-tickle torture the fuck out of me!!! Ha, ha, ha, ha, ha, ha, ha, ha, ha, ha, ha, ha, ha!!!!!"

As he laughed and spoke in between his bouts of laughter his breath stunk of the rancid piss he had just drunk and the marijuana he had been smoking. I ran the paintbrush bristles up and down and up and down the beefy bottoms of his big feet. His feet twitched and jerked in the confines if the device.

"Hoooooo, ha, ha, ha, ha, ha, ha, ha, h-how am I goin' to do business with you after this shit bud?" Sean Curtis asked me. "How the fuck can I do business with a guy who tickle tortured me, jacked me the fuck off and…and…made me drink piss, ha, ha, ha, ha, ha, ha, ha, ha, ha, ha, ha, ha!!!!!!"

"Lets not forget that I kissed you too Curtis," I added, paint brushing and paint brushing the bottoms of his bare feet.

"F-faggot that you are man!!!" he chortled. "Ha, ha, ha, ha, ha, ha, ha, ha, ha, ha, ha, ha!!!!!!"

I used the paintbrushes on his feet for a good half-hour. At that point I estimated that we had been down there in the boiler room for close to three hours or so. Sean Curtis looked like one sweaty and real beat to shit football jock as he sat there gasping again for breath in between being tickled.

"Ar-are we done now bud?" he asked me.

"Not quite," I said as I stroked his cock a few times. "I need you to shoot another load for me because I want you real sensitive and ornery for the great conclusion to all this. And for that conclusion we'll need the blindfold again…"

He whimpered and gasped miserably as I stroked him slowly toward another jock boy gusher…

"Faggot, that's what I've been snagged by here, a real faggot," he grunted and then looked up at the ceiling as if searching for Heaven. "Ohhhhhrrrrr god man, c-can't believe I'm about to shoot my damned load a third fucking time…ohhhhhhrrrrr yeahhhhhhh!!!!!"

His Adam's apple bobbed big and pronounced in his throat as I squeezed his third load of jock boy sperm from him, splattering it again all over his massive chest area. He grunted, groaned and swore like a captured marine as I worked his cock and he spewed his mess. His body twitched magnificently in the bondage as I gave his now overly sensitive cock a few last tugs, getting the last droplets of cum from him...

A few moments later the tied up muscle boy was blindfolded again as I reached into my bag of tricks for the last time that day...

I brought out two long back massagers, AKA women's vibrators...

With that maniacal look in my eyes again I clicked the things on and looked at my blindfolded, high and beat to tickle shit jock boy...

"Und now for zee great finale'," I said to him in an old time director's accent.

I slowly and methodically worked the long vibrators under his arms, pressing them up against his hairless armpits.

"OHHHHHHHHHHHHH noooooooooooo!!!!!" he wailed and his jaw seemed to drop as there was no way he could get the vibrators out from under his arms because of the way he was tied up to the pipes behind him. "HAAAARRRRRhhhhhhh, ha, ha, ha, ha, ha, ha, ha, ha, ha, ha, ha, ha, ha, ha, ha, ha, ha!!!!!!"

As the vibrators purred and whirred at a high speed I settled down at my trapped jock boy's locked up feet and took one of them tightly in my hands... As his raunchy armpits were tickle tortured I licked and slurped at the bottoms of his stinky feet, sucked his toes and slid my tongue over his arches...

The muscle boy laughed and laughed and laughed and laughed and laughed....

Four and a half hours later Sean Curtis and I emerged from the boiler room, I looking none the worse for the time spent down there, he on the other hand looking totally exhausted and mind-clouded.

"Okay, you've got a supply of smoke to last you a week Curtis," I said to him as he stood there wearing just his gym shorts and sneakers without socks, his tee shirt still stuck in the back pocket of his shorts. "Be here next week at this time and I'll have the next supply for you."

"Be *h-here?*" he asked me, glancing with fear down the steps of the boiler room.

"Well, only if you want the stuff at the discount price," I said. "If you want to pay full price and not use the relaxation device that's up to you bud."

He looked at me miserably, turned and trudged away. I stood there watching his magnificently muscular back as he walked off, holding his raunchy sweat socks in my hand…

"Hey there buddy," I heard a voice call out to me.

I glanced to my side and saw the custodian from the campus.

"Looks like you got a new customer and a new victim for your device down in the boiler room," he said to me as I handed him a few bills. "Let me know when you'll need the boiler room again and I'll make myself scarce again for you."

"Same time next week bud, same time next week," I murmured, holding tight to Sean Curtis' socks…

A Boner Book

Shining The Police Rookie's Shoes

"Hey buddy, got time to do one more shine job?" I heard the deep guttural voice ask from behind me.

His last name was Carassco, according to the nametag pinned to his tight fitting uniform shirt, (tight fitting because he was totally muscular and well toned, built like a brick house) Police Rookie Carassco to be exact.

"Uh yes, I suppose I do," I said after I turned around, taking in the glorious sight of the smooth domed (skin headed) handsome young New York police rookie, standing in the doorway of my shoe shining booth in Penn Station.

His uniform consisted of a gray short sleeved button down shirt, a thin black tie, dark blue uniform trousers with a black silk stripe down the sides of the legs, and black lace-up shoes. His nametag that read "Carrasco" was pinned onto the top of his shirt pocket, right over where his left sided nipple would be. I wondered fleetingly and in my fantasies if the pin of that nametag was skewered through his nipple underneath his shirt. What a sight that would be I thought. His felt police rookie hat was neatly folded over and tucked under his belt. If he looked great in his police rookie uniform I could only imagine how he would fill out the navy blue one he would be issued when he graduated the academy. It was actually a couple of minutes to seven in the evening, seven o'clock being the time that I close my booth in the Penn Station Concourse for the night. Any executives still in the city at seven o'clock are not thinking about getting their shoes shined. They're thinking of getting home, seeing as they've more than likely been working overtime at that point. My big rush of business usually happens between the hours of seven to nine AM, when all those handsome execs are on their way in to their offices. So as I said, at seven PM I am usually all set to close up shop for the night; but at the sight of this handsome young man in his police rookie uniform I have to admit that my breath caught in my throat. And not to mention that I wanted more than anything to get down near his feet to shine his big shoes.

"I mean, it looks like you're getting ready to close up for the night," the rookie said, pointing at the drawer in the cabinet where I had just deposited a few shoe shining brushes. "I don't want to keep you from your wife or girlfriend you know…"

"It's not a problem," I said with a smile, wondering why he thought I had wife or a girlfriend. "Please, come in, hop up in a chair, and make yourself comfortable, please."

"Thanks man," he said, lugging his oversized police issued luggage-like bag with him as he entered my booth.

He was approximately five feet nine inches tall, smooth domed, as I already pointed out (skinhead), he had intense looking dark brown eyes, (actually his eyes had a look of total determination in them) a light olive complexion and I guessed his age to be in the very early twenties. Most New York City police recruits are around that age. As he placed his bag on the floor I was able to see the muscles in his wide back pressing against his uniform shirt, straining to free themselves from the confines of it, it seemed. The muscles in his upper arms bulged and flexed as he'd lugged his bag along, the thick rope-like veins showing real paramount in his bowling ball like biceps and his thick forearms thanks to his short sleeved uniform shirt. I wondered if when issuing uniforms it had been difficult to find a shirt that would fit this muscle boy. I imagined that he worked out with weights probably every day of the week.

"Any chair is okay?" he asked as he faced me, loosening his thin black tie and unbuttoning his top shirt button.

"The one on the end is fine," I said, pointing at the chair that was up on the raised shoe shining platform.

He walked real macho like, almost shuffling over to the chair, hoisted himself up and sat down comfortably in it, settling his muscular body down in a relaxed posture, resting his big shoes on the footrests in front of him.

"Do you mind if I put up my "Closed" sign Officer?" I asked him. "You will be the last customer for the day."

"Nah, I don't mind," he replied, grabbing his uniform trousers at the knees and hiking them up to his calves, showing a lot of black sock, exposing his shoes for the shine to come. "It's nice of you to call me "Officer" buddy, although I won't be a full-fledged cop for another few months or so, that's when I graduate the academy."

"That's okay, I'll call you officer anyway," I said with my back to him.

I hung my "Closed" sign on the outside of the door of my booth and then very slowly closed the door...

"Ah fuck, look at that," the tuff boy police rookie said, staring down at his feet as I turned back to face him.

"Something the matter?" I asked him, thinking he was perturbed that I had closed the door to the booth.

"Yeah, something is the matter all right, fuck, I got a smudge on my left shoe; that fucking dork on the train that ran past me stepped right on my foot," he said angrily as I slowly made my way over to him. "People can be so rude. God damn it all, just because that lanky suit guy was in a rush didn't give him the right to step on my goddamned shoe! Fuck, when I'm a full-fledged cop if I see someone do that I'll issue them a goddamned ticket. Now I'm really glad I decided to get my shoes shined before heading home."

I stood in front of him and looked down at the smudge he was talking about.

"Not to worry Officer," I said, trying not to be so breathless as I stared at his exquisite looking feet as he dangled them at the sides of the footrests, still taking in the sight of the offending smudge on his left shoe. "I'll be able to get that smudge out for you."

I guessed his feet to be around size eleven to twelve or thereabouts.

"And as always my damned socks are drooping down," he went on angrily. "Do me a favor will you buddy, pull my socks up for me before you get started shining up my shoes huh?"

My jaw nearly dropped. At the sound of that request my breath actually did catch in my throat. Never before in all the years that I had been shining (mostly guys) shoes did a customer request that I pull his socks up for him. Many times over my shoe shining years I had been tempted to pull up those young studly Wall Street guy's socks while they would sit for an early morning shine. Or how about the sailor's and soldier's on leave during the summer months in New York City; how many times I was tempted to give their dress socks a tug or two to yank them up for them while they sat for a shine. There really is something erotic and unnerving about pulling a studly guy's socks up for him, especially if you're a shoe shine guy or even a shoe salesman. You would more than likely be very surprised by guy's reactions as they watch their socks being yanked up by another guy. Now I had a muscular hunk requesting such a thing and not just a muscular hunk, but a muscular hunk of a police rookie.

"Uh, of course Sir, no problem at all," I said, stepping closer to him as he again rested his feet on the footrests.

I gingerly reached under the bottoms of his hiked up uniform trousers, found the top of his left black nylon dress sock and slowly pulled it up for him, hiking his uniform trousers up even more as I went. His socks were wide ribbed, my personal favorites, as I pulled up the first one for him I took note of the fact that they were also OTC, over the calf if you would. Not many young guys these days favor OTC socks, but I was sure glad that this handsome police rookie did. There really is something very erotic about a young muscular guy wearing a pair of black OTC nylon dress socks. After I was done pulling up his left sock I quickly rolled his uniform pants leg up higher, folding it as I went, that way I would not get shoe polish on his trousers when I started working on his shoes.

"Thanks man, someday someone is going to invent dress socks that stay up and don't droop so much," the police rookie said, watching as I reached under the bottom of his right sided pant leg and grabbed the top of that sock next.

"I find that white sweat socks stay up better than dress socks," I commented as I slowly pulled his right sided sock up for him.

"Yeah, I know what you mean buddy," the police rookie said in his deep voice. "I think the manufacturers put more elastic in white sweat socks. But we can't wear white sweat socks with the rookie uniform. Actually, can you believe that they tell us that? I mean fuck, full fledged cops can wear shoe boots with white sweat socks with their uniforms, but when rookies are issued their uniforms we're told by our superior officers that we have to purchase black lace-up shoes and to be sure that our socks are black."

I finished pulling his right sided sock up for him, folded up his pants leg some more, and then stepped back and again took in the glorious sight of him. He looked totally majestic and somehow humble at the same time as he sat on my raised chair with his big feet resting on the footrests, his uniform pants hiked way up and showing off a lot of black sock, sort of like a handsome prince on his throne. His size of ham hands gripped the armrests. His hands actually looked big and strong enough to punch holes through walls with.

"I think Officer, that part of the reason you have a problem with your thin dress socks staying up is that your calves are very muscular," I said to him, sounding a bit sheepish. "I uh, noticed that when my knuckles were rubbing against them when I pulled your socks up for you just now. Perhaps your calves are too muscular for the thin socks and that's why they droop. But again, white sweat socks do seem to be made with more elastic in them, more than likely for the reason I just mentioned."

"Well, being a jock at heart I guess I have to admit that I didn't own any damn black dressy socks," the police rookie said as I took a shoe shining cloth from a drawer. "All my socks were thick whites, you know what I mean buddy?"

"I sure do," I said with a smile and began expertly buffing his shoes with the shoe shine cloth.

"It was when I decided to join the police force that I realized I would need black socks," he went on.

He looked downward as I buffed his shoes...

"So it was a good thing that my dad works for a bank," he went on, watching as I buffed his shoes with the cloth, preparing them for shining. "I borrowed a couple of pairs of his banker's socks, ha, what he calls his executive socks."

So that explained the OTCs he was wearing. Most bankers do prefer OTC dress socks after all…

"Got to tell you though man, it felt weird at first you know, wearing my dad's socks," he chuckled as I finished the buff job on his shoes, having gotten all the dust off them before getting ready for the task of shining them.

My hands were still sort of shaking after having pulled the rookie's socks up for him…

"Listen to me here buddy, ha, going on and on about my dad's executive socks and having to wear them with my uniform," the rookie said.

"It's not a problem Sir," I said, fingering the smudge on his shoe. "I'll have that out for you in no time Sir…"

"Yeah, so anyway, dear old Dad lent me a few pairs of his black dressy socks and then I bought a few pairs for myself when I went to buy those shoes I'm wearing," Rookie Carassco still went on, seeming to be enjoying talking about his socks for some reason. "Although I didn't buy the ones like my dad lent me. I bought the ones that just come up to my calves. Dear old dad seems to relish his socks up to his knees. Guess you can tell I got a pair of dad's socks on today huh?"

"Yes Sir," I replied and began using another cloth, a softer one this time to begin working on the smudge on the police rookie's shoe.

"And the stink man," he said to me with a grin.

"Th-the stink Sir?" I asked him.

"Yeah, the way my dressy socks stink at the end of the day," he said. "Fuck, when I take those dress socks off they stink worse than my sweat socks do after I've played a game of basketball with my buddies or worked out at the gym. Can't explain it buddy, they just stink like crazy."

"Well, it could be because dress socks are a lot thinner than sweat socks and they don't absorb the sweat as much," I said, trying to explain without sounding breathless why the rookie's socks stunk at the end of a long day. "And also the leather of your shoes can cause your socks to smell that way as well…"

As I spoke I rubbed and rubbed with my cloth at the smudge on the rookie's shoe. To my surprise and to the rookie's irritation the smudge started getting worse, spreading somehow, rather than disappearing...

"Fuck man, look at that shit, you're making it worse," the angered police rookie said, looking down at the smudge as it now spread.

"I-I'm sorry Sir," I stammered. "I didn't mean to..."

"Don't you know how to do spit polish?" he asked me brusquely.

"S-spit polish Sir?" I replied nervously.

"Yeah, fucking spit polish, like the military guys do," he said to me, looking down at me as if I was stupid.

"Uh, I suppose so Sir," I said.

"Before my dad got the job at the bank he was in the army for four years," the rookie told me. "While he was in the army he was taught to spit polish his dress shoes. All guys in the military have to know how to spit shine their shoes. Fuck, if the sergeant can't see his reflection in your shoes at inspection time you're in a shit load of trouble my dad told me."

"Uh, of course Sir," I responded dutifully. "One spit shine coming up."

I quickly took a clean cloth from my supply drawer; with my hands slightly shaking I folded it into a small square and spit on it a few times, dribbling actually to get it good and moist. Rookie Carassco looked down at me with an expression on his face which said that he could not believe what he was seeing.

"What the fuck are you doing buddy?" the rookie asked me. "Did I come to the wrong shoe shining booth or what?"

"Sir?" I replied, looking up at him with a quizzical look on my face, holding the moistened cloth in my hand.

"Spit shine, *spit shine*," he said, definitely sounding angry now. "Read my lips man, Spit...fucking...shine..."

He looked at me with his eyes practically blazing in his smooth domed head...

"Y-you mean you want me to spit on your shoes Officer?" I asked him nervously.

"Finally, we're getting somewhere," the police rookie said, sounding relieved. "Yes, spit on my shoes and then you'll be able to get that smudge off them. Fuck, I cannot believe that I'm teaching you how to do your job here."

"Y-yes Sir, one spit shine coming up," I repeated.

I put down the cloth that I had just spit on and leaned over awkwardly, trying to get my lips and tongue down near the rookie's shoes to be able to spit on them.

"Oh man, this is fucking unbelievable," the rookie said then, sounding even more irritated. "All this just to get a smudge off my shoe. Buddy, you'll never balance yourself that way…"

Again I looked up at him and said, "Sir?"

"Grab my calves," he said to me. "Grab them real tight and then you'll be balanced in that bent over position, then you can spit on my shoes and get busy spit shining them… If not we're going to be here all fucking night…"

"Y-yes Sir," I said nervously. "G-grab your calves, yes Sir!"

"Yep, you got it, grab my goddamned calves," the muscular rookie said, sweat seeming to form and glisten atop his skinhead dome. "The ones that cause my dressy socks to droop so much, according to you…"

With my hands more than trembling at that point I gripped his black socked calves tightly and then leaned forward and slowly bent over again. The muscles in his calves felt like iron under his thin nylon dress socks let me tell you.

"Good, good, now we're getting somewhere," he said in a deep throaty sounding voice. "Now, a few good liberal spits on each shoe and then you can start polishing them up for me…"

I leaned down further, wanting to hold onto his socked calves forever it seemed. His socks felt so warm against his muscular and well toned calves that I had all to do to keep myself from running my hands up and down them. I wanted to droop his socks down and pull them back up again and again…

"What are you doing down there buddy?" the rookie asked me, sounding totally gruff.

Looking up at him quickly but not letting go of his calves I asked him, "Sir?"

"I told you to grip my calves so you could balance yourself man," he said, practically sneering at me. "That way you could get busy spit shining my shoes. I didn't say to stare at my black dressy socks like they were the greatest thing since the invention of the wheel…"

"Y-yes Sir, I mean no Sir," I said and quickly lowered my eyes back down to his shoes.

As I looked back down I could not help quickly taking in the sight of the massive bulge that he was sporting in the crotch area of his uniform trousers. Somehow the hunky and studly police rookie was enjoying this scene of domination and humiliation that had somehow begun in my shoe shining booth. Needless to say I was enjoying it as well… Heeding his orders I held his socked calves real tight, leaned down further with my mouth directly over the tops of his shoes and worked up a good mess of saliva in my mouth. Slowly and carefully I dribbled a bit and then spit sprightly onto his shoe tops. My saliva dripped to the sides of his shoes and ran liberally over the tops of them. He wriggled his toes in his shoes.

"Good man," the hunky police rookie said, sounding proud. "Again now…"

I gripped his socked calves tighter still, worked up more saliva in my mouth and spit and dribbled again onto his shoes. My lips were actually close enough to kiss his shoes and believe you me I was very tempted to do just that bud…

"Okay, one more time and then you should be able to start polishing them up," Rookie Carassco said, sounding a little more patient now.

Holding his black socked calves tighter yet I worked up more saliva in my mouth and again spit and dribbled liberally all over his shoes.

"Good, good," the rookie said, sounding glad. "Now, use your tongue to swirl your saliva all over the tops and sides of my shoes. And don't forget about the sides of my heels either man!"

I held his calves tight and a feeling of disbelief coursed through me…

"M-my tongue Sir?" I asked him, not looking up at him, instead staring at his black wide ribbed socks as I held his calves.

"Sure thing buddy, what were you thinking about?" the rookie asked me and I swear I could feel him grinning sadistically down at me.

"Well Officer, I was thinking that I would use a clean cloth and buff my spit, er, my saliva off your shoes," I said, speaking as my lips grazed the laces of his shoe that my face was near, inhaling the musky scent of his sock at the same time.

"Then it wouldn't be a spit shine would it?" he asked me, again sounding as if he thought I was stupid.

"No Sir, I suppose it wouldn't be at that," I replied.

"Good, now, hold onto my calves real tight and stick out your tongue," the rookie instructed me. "Can't believe I'm leading you through this every fucking step of the way. I get the feeling you'll have to pay me when you're done."

I smiled for a moment and chuckled before sticking out my tongue.

I started swirling my tongue over his left sided shoe first, moving the tip of it over and over and through the mess of my saliva on his shoe.

"Good, really apply as much pressure to it as you can," he said to me. "Most people don't know the strength they have in their tongues."

I could feel him looking forward and downward as I tongued his shoe. At one point I pressed my pursed lips against the smudge on his shoe that had started all this and dribbled some more on it before getting to the task of tonguing it.

"Now you got it buddy," the rookie said with total approval in his voice, reached down and ruffled my hair.

I glanced up at him for a second and his handsome face was lit up in a smile that could brighten a room. I also took note again of the bulge he was sporting in his uniform pants.

As I swirled my tongue over the spit moistened smudge on his shoe it finally began to dissipate.

"There you go," the rookie said proudly. "Now you got it man, spit polish those shoes of mine!!"

"Yes Sir," I said my lips against his shoe as I spoke.

"Don't forget the sides of them and the sides of the heels as well buddy," he said to me with total authority as I lapped at the top of his shoe.

"I won't forget Sir," I said.

Slowly, I moved my tongue away from where the smudge had been and even licked cleaned the part of the tongue of his shoe that was visible. As I did that my nose was pressed against his black nylon sock. I inhaled deeply; he heard me…

"Fuck man, again with my socks huh?" he asked me, leaning back in the chair and looking down at me, seeming to mull something over. "I really get the feeling you got a thing for my dressy socks buddy."

"Y-you think so Sir?" I asked him as I trailed my tongue along the side of his shoe, holding his foot aloft off the footrest by the calf as I did so.

My nose pressed against his socked ankle and again he heard me inhale the scent of his long black sock.

By now I was sweating like crazy, both from the fact that the booth was small and the door was closed and from the fact that I was in a state of sheer ecstasy… With his foot held aloft in my hand I did as he had instructed me and ran my tongue along the side of the heel of his shoe. It smelled a bit funky and I knew that my tongue was going to be a mess by the time all this was over. I did the same thing with his other foot, cleaning my saliva off his shoe bit by bit with my tongue, inhaling the scent of his other sock as well.

"Fucking shoe shining guy," the muscular rookie said snidely with a mean looking grin on his face at that point. "Of all things, you got a goddamned thing for my smelly dressy socks! I wonder how my dad would feel if he knew I had a shoe shine guy sniffin' his socks!"

A short while later I was done spit shining the rookie's shoes. They looked as good as new and my tongue felt very tired indeed. As he looked down at his shoes as his feet rested atop the footrests I reluctantly let go of his ankles.

"Not bad, not bad at all," he said to me, inspecting his newly shined shoes more than thoroughly. "Now, let me tell me what I was thinking bud…"

"Sir?" I asked him as he looked at me very wickedly.

"Seeing as you definitely got a thing for my socks here I think it's only right that you should clean them up for me as well buddy," the ruggedly handsome police rookie said to me, still with that wicked look in his eyes.

"S-Sir?" I asked him nervously.

"Carefully, and remember I said carefully buddy, carefully take my shoes of my feet and then you can get busy working that stink I mentioned earlier out of my dad's socks for me," the rookie said commandingly.

He leaned back in the chair and crossed his hands up behind his smooth dome…

"Y-you want me to spit polish your socks as well Sir?" I asked him as I slowly and gingerly unlaced his shoelaces.

"Fuck that buddy, I want you to suck the stink out of them," he chuckled as I slowly and gently, careful not to smudge them again slid his shoes off his feet.

The scent that emanated from his black socked feet was musky and overpoweringly sexy at the same time…

I placed his shoes up on a shelf and then faced him. I took a deep breath, gripped his calves and leaned down to get to work. He wiggled his toes as I sucked them into my mouth…

"Oh man, great idea this was to come here tonight," the rookie muttered with satisfaction. "Not only will my shoes be nice and shined up for tomorrow but my girl won't complain tonight when I get home and take my shoes off. Fucking bitch hates the way my dressy socks stink. Hey buddy, while you're at it down there pull my socks up again for me will you? They seem to have drooped down again…

Badge # 28754

"AYYYYRRRRRRRRR!!!!!! *Shit!!!! Shit!!!!* Stop it, *stop this now!!!!* F-fuck it all you damned sleazy law breakers!!! My goddamned tits aren't for you guys to be fucking making sport out of sucking and slurping and chewing on!!!" I panted madly and in a full rage, stupidly trapped in the back alley of an abandoned apartment building. "You fuck heads will pay for this, mark my words!!!"

I realized I sounded like a bad old-time movie. There wasn't much else I could think of saying in my defense, as I was being violated in such fashions.

"Pay for it Offisair Mach? I don't think so, seeing as we're getting it all for free, and I don't know about that other thing you just spat shit about either," one of the thugs chortled meanly, his mouth off my poor swollen and sore man tit for the moment, the palm of one of his big hands resting on my ass cheeks, squeezing and kneading a handful of my delectable globes. "Because judging from the present situation, *your* present situation, *that is* just what these big fat juicy tits of yours are for!!"

That said he gave my rear end a tight squeeze, getting me involuntarily to my tiptoes for a moment.

"Faggot!!" I seethed in his face.

"Now, now, Offisair, a good cop doesn't pass judgment that way," he said, squeezing and squeezing my ass cheek good and hard, so hard that I could feel the bruise that I would have there come the next day. "And besides, you don't need to be a faggot to enjoy *a really good* pair of tits."

With that he greedily slurped my big nub of a man tit back into his mouth, wrapping his thick lips around it, clamping it meanly with his front teeth and slurping and chewing at it madly. His tongue tip teased and teased the tip of my overly erect nub as he sucked it with wild abandon.

"Fuck it all you guys, *I am an officer of the law!! A police officer, a uniform and badge wearing police officer no less! And what you two law breakers are doing is totally and one hundred percent against the law!!*" I ranted bitterly and angrily. "Not to mention the fact that you've kidnapped me!"

"Yeah, lets not mention it," the other thug laughed and he gave my exposed and semi hard manhood a good squeeze and a twirl. "Wonder what this is for. Is this for us not to be sucking and slurping on too Offisair? But I bet you'd like that huh? Bet you'd love for us to suck your little baton huh?"

"AYYYYYRRRRR good Gods, l-leave my damned cock alone you pervert!" I seethed through clenched teeth.

He smiled sadistically up at me, bent down at my other man tit and gave my manhood a few tugs before letting go of the guy. Now I was a bit more than semi hard, I was almost up to pledging allegiance. Droplets of pre seed oozed from my wide sexy slit and dripped down onto the tops of my black old fashioned rubber soled police issued shoes. Fuck, fuck, I could not believe that they had squeezed two good gushy loads out of me already. There was no damned doubt in my mind that they would want more real fucking soon. Chuckling meanly the other guy did as his buddy had just done, namely slurping and sucking and bighting my poor man tits for more than an hour at that point. Fucking thugs really loved a good meaty pair of tits that was for sure. Staring straight ahead I looked miserably and with a feeling of despair at the stains on the red brick wall in front of us, the embarrassing and telltale stains of my cop slop, my cum from the two times that the two jokers had viciously jacked me off. And judging from the present situation and what the second thug had just said they were far from done with my cock either…

I stood there in the early evening of a hot New York night, totally helpless and feeling totally fucking stupid. My dark blue police uniform shirt and tie were off me along with my white tee shirt; my big, muscular, hairy chest bared real paramount for the two thugs to have a field day with. And boy howdy that's exactly what they were doing man, treating my tits like they were the tits of a cheap and sleazy whore. Actually, my uniform shirt, my tie and my tee shirt were hanging nearby on a low rail of the fire escape. My hands were locked behind me, with my own handcuffs I might add, sadly of course (the damned cuffs were bighting meanly into the skin on my wrists they had them snapped on me so damned tight.) Nothing is more humiliating for a cop than to wind up locked in his own handcuffs, let me tell you… My utility belt along with my gun and baton were on the ground just below the fire escape, totally out of my reach. What I wouldn't have given at that moment to get my hands on my gun… My radio was turned off, no way of contacting help even if I could get to it, and because I was off duty no one at headquarters was going to wonder why Badge number 28754 was out of radio contact. I would think that after this incident that cops would be required to leave their radios on at all times, even while off duty. Cops were always targets for thugs like these, and thugs like these had very cleverly captured yours truly here. My muscular and well-developed upper arms were tightly roped at my bowling-ball sized biceps, forcing my huge arms further and painfully behind me. The rope was squeezing my biceps a tad more than painfully I might add here. My pride and joy, namely my big fat and long juicy cock was hanging out of the fly opening of my uniform trousers along with my egg sized balls. As pointed out already I was now a little more than semi hard and my cock was all slimy with the remnants of my earlier messes as the two thugs ate and chomped like crazy on my big ol' man tits. Thick droplets of pre seed oozed more and more from my wide sexy slit. Damn, I am straight as a goddamned arrow so what was up with that shit anyhow??? Why was my damned cock betraying me that way bud? Then, again, the two thugs stopped eating my tits and they each grabbed one of my big upper arms.

"Okay Offisair, let's see you do it again!" the first thug said, grabbing a handful of my sexy bubble butt as they moved me close to the wall. "I would say enough time has gone by for you to have cooked up some more cop soup for us…"

"Oh no, *no,* not this shit again you guys!" I pleaded and panted miserably. "Fuck it all you two, but th-this is a shitty thing to be doing to an officer of the law!"

Ignoring me they forced me up to my tiptoes and then took turns tugging and jerking my big manhood and stealing squeezes at my big tender and juicy balls. I might add for the report how they weren't all that gentle in the way they handled me. They wringed my cock with their fists, making it feel real sore as they went after tugging and jerking on it. And my balls, well, anything after a gentle squeeze on a poor guy's balls would have to be defined as painful bud. But I had been right, they *were* planning on getting more cop slop out of me, to further humiliate me it would seem. It worked this way, whoever had me in hand when I shot my load got to give me a big wet sloppy kiss right on the damned lips after I was done jazzing. And fuck of fucks, *there wasn't shit that I could do to stop the two mangy thugs from feasting on me like I was a damned buffet!*

As they took turns tugging my manhood and squeezing my poor aching balls I looked down at my overly erect swollen nipples. They were sticking out on my chest like two bullets... Fuck, I had never thought my man tits, let alone *anyone's tits* could ever be that erect, that swollen and that wrecked looking. Looking down I quickly thought back to how I had come to be in this sickening mess...

My name is Mach, Officer Steve Mach to be exact. I'm twenty-seven years old, been on the New York City police force for five years now. For the record *I'm a damned good cop!* I'm black African on my mother's side and white Irish on my father's side, which adds up to my mulatto colored skin. I have big brown eyes and dark brown hair, cut short in a very severe military look, tantamount to a marine. I'm six feet tall and built good and fucking muscular like a real kick-ass marine. The day that I'm relating herein had been just like any other, except that this particular day ended with me being kidnapped by two mangy thugs and having said thugs work over my man tits like two guys who hadn't had tits in more than a few months. I'm a foot beat officer in a pretty seedy area of New York City. I was at the end of my shift for that day and let me tell you bud my feet were killing me. Walking around city blocks, subway trains and stations can really do a number on a cop's feet. That's why I wear those old fashioned rubbed soled shoes rather than those big military like clonky boots that so many of my cop brothers prefer nowadays. After radioing in that I was going off duty I turned off my radio and was about to head back to headquarters when I noticed a homeless man wrapped in blankets sleeping in the alley behind an abandoned and soon to be thrown down apartment building. Fuck it all I thought miserably. All I was thinking about at that moment was getting home, getting my shoes and smelly black socks off and submerging my size eleven tired cop feet in a basin filled with hot water and some peppermint foot lotion from the Body Shop. Ah well, this wouldn't take all that long I thought. I didn't even bother to radio in to headquarters to let them know that I was making one final check for the day. As I said my radio was turned off. When I got to where the homeless man was sleeping I squatted down on my haunches and poked him with two fingertips.

"Hey bud," I said, poking him some more, trying to get him to wake up. "Come on man, you can't be sleeping back here."

The first thing that I noticed to be sort of strange was the fact that like most other homeless people this guy didn't reek of a foul odor. The second thing I noticed was the fact that his blankets appeared to be brand new. The third thing that went through my mind was the fact that it was really hot that day and this guy was wrapped in a blanket.

"Mmmmmm," the guy murmured, as he seemed to be waking up.

He slowly turned over and I saw that he was young, very young. Shit, he couldn't be more than twenty-one or twenty-two years old.

"Wh-what happened?" the guy asked, bringing a hand out from under the blanket.

"You okay bud?" I asked him.

At the sight of me he smiled meanly from ear to ear, seeming to drink in the sight of me. I felt a chill crawl up my spine…

"Hello Offisair," he whispered and before I realized what he was about to do he slammed his hand against my face and squeezed tight.

"H-hey!!!! HEY!!!" I gasped and then with total brute force he pushed me backward on my haunches.

I stumbled backward, somehow got to my feet, and the guy grabbed me from behind by my uniform shirt collar. He yanked it up and threw me forward bodily; I went stumbling and was slammed hard against the brick wall of the apartment building.

"OOOOFFFFFF!!!!!" I sputtered as my muscular back and shoulders took most of the blow, seeing as I had managed to turn myself around a bit as I was thrown.

"Come on out Carlos!" the guy shouted, shedding his blanket.

From around the corner of the alley a second guy appeared. He quickly grabbed one of my upper arms and punched me a good hard one right in the ol' gut.

"UUUHHHFFFFFF!!!" I grunted, totally startled, the wind literally knocked out of me.

He punched me again.

"HHHOOOFFFFF!!!" I grunted again, this time almost jumping out of my damned shoes he'd gut punched me so hard.

And again he punched me, and again, and again, really getting me coughing, retching a bit and sputtering in the sudden onslaught of pain that I was being dealt. With my other hand I went for my gun but the guy who had been on the ground just seconds ago was there to stop me. With his body he held my arm against the brick wall. They stood at my sides taking turns punching and jabbing me harder and harder in the gut, over and over and over and over again. When I was totally wracked with pain and more than doubled over and standing before the two young thugs with my arms wrapped over my stomach I realized that during the battering I had been given I had also been relieved of my utility belt, my gun, my baton and my radio. I was coughing, gagging, and dizzy with the pain from the awful beating I had just endured. Massive globs of phlegm, saliva and even some blood were hacked up from my gut. I spit miserably onto the ground, trying desperately to catch even one good breath.

F-fffffucking b-bastards, hell of a way to treat a cop," I blubbered amid the mess coming out of my mouth with every word I spoke.

From behind me one of the thugs gave me a hard kick on the ass. I stumbled forward stupidly...

"Come on Offisair, *get back there!*" he said meanly, kicking me again in the ass, and again, kicking me around the corner of the alley, thus concealing us from any passerby that might happen along.

When I was kicked again I had no choice but to move along as I had been instructed to. The bastard kicked me again and again across the sexy ass and with my arms looped over my stomach area I moved along slowly and more stupidly. Once we were behind the building the two young thugs grabbed my arms and pulled me to a standing position.

"AAARRHHHHHH!!!!" I roared as the awful pain shot through my stomach area.

I dribbled up more saliva and it ran embarrassingly down the front of my uniform shirt. The two thugs then yanked my arms meanly behind me, getting my chest jutted out and real sexy looking for their perverted pleasures. My uniform shirt clung tightly and erotically to my muscular torso.

"AAARRRHHHHH, shhhiittt!!!" I roared in pain anew as they forced my huge and muscular arms behind me.

"Fuck man, holy fucking shit Carlos, look at that!!" the first thug said breathlessly to the guy who had punched me first in the stomach. "Two nice big fat tits! Fuck man, just like I predicted. God fucking almighty man, I can always tell just by looking at somebody if they have a good pair of tits."

Needless to say my man tits were pressing seductively against my uniform shirt, enticing the two young thugs more and more it seemed. Fuck, they both couldn't have been more than twenty-two years old or there around, let me tell you. The one named Carlos was obviously Spanish. He had dark silky wavy hair mean looking brown eyes and was just slightly shorter than I. His buddy, the one who had posed as a homeless man to lure me into the alley, was a crew cut blond with piercing blue eyes and he was also slightly shorter than I was. Well, shorter than I or not, these two street thugs had gotten the drop and the goods on good old Officer Mach.

"Come on Carlos, let's get this fucking side of beef cop shirtless and start eating," the blond guy said lecherously. "Dinner is served and the only goddamned thing on the menu is cop tits."

Laughing, the two young men stripped me of my uniform shirt and tie. Shit, the thought of these two guys, *or any two guys for that matter referring to my tits like they were dinner was enough to get me a little better than pissed the fuck off,* let me tell you.

"H-hey, come on now you two, th-this has gone far enough!!" I grunted angrily as they got my uniform shirt, my tie and literally tore my white cotton tee shirt off me.

As I was de-uniformed on top I tried to struggle away from them, but the pain in my gut was still too much. I didn't feel like risking being punched there again. I felt that if they gut punched me again everything that was inside me would come gushing up out of my mouth, not a pretty sight for an officer of the law.

"It hasn't even begun Offisair," the blond guy said, holding up my damned handcuffs.

Before I even realized it my hands were locked behind me. Nothing is worse for a cop than being locked in his own handcuffs. Then, Carlos wallowed joyfully in the task of tying my upper arms tightly together with a length of rope that he'd had in his jeans pocket.

"F-fuckingguysman,*th-thisshitisagainstthelaw!!*"I garbled miserably and then to my utter shock the two thugs leaned down at my big chest and slurped one of my fleshy and over-sized man tits each into their greedy mouths. "OHHHHHRRRRR, good gods, *oh you fucking perverts!!* Wh-what is this shit??? Just what the fucking fuck is going on here???" As they slurped and sucked heartily at my big man-sized tits I felt myself rising embarrassingly to the occasion in my uniform trousers.

"Fucking lawbreakers, let me go you guys!!" I ranted madly, curling my cuffed hands into tight fists and my tied biceps straining helplessly in the tight bondage.

They held me tightly in place by my hips, their hands dangerously close to my crotch area. The sounds of slurping and sucking filled the deserted area behind the abandoned apartment building. It was the sound of my cop tits being eaten for dinner by the two young thugs.

"Bastards, you are both under arrest as of this moment," I complained bitterly, feeling totally violated. "And if you two know what's good for you, you will release me and take that arrest I just imposed on you very seriously."

"Start reading us our rights Offisair," the blond guy laughed.

"*I said you are both under arrest,*" I seethed. "Your rights will be read to you once my rights as an officer of the law have been re-established."

In response the two young thugs each reached around me, grabbed one of my ass cheeks each and slurped harder and harder and with real gusto on my poor man tits.

"AAARRRRRGGGHHH," I ranted and involuntarily lifted myself to my tiptoes.

I writhed and squirmed, feeling angry and humiliated as the two young thugs ate my tits…

"Mmmmmmm, best fucking tits I've had in a while," the blond thug said to his buddy and quickly slurped my nub back into his greedy mouth.

They each squeezed my bubble shaped ass cheeks, further humiliating the fuck out of me, making me dance and squirm stupidly for them up on my tiptoes. They slurped harder and harder on my man tits, causing me to clench my teeth in (ecstasy?) pain.

"You fucking blasted mugs had better stop this shit now," I ranted. "Any minute now a bunch of my cop buddies are going to be here."

"Oh no they're not Offisair," the blond guy chuckled, taking his mouth temporarily off my man tit and squeezing my ass cheek tighter, inflicting real pain back there let me tell you. "You are an off duty police offisair, your radio being turned off attests to that shit. *You are our pussy for the duration.*"

"Hey Dennis, I have a really great fucking idea," Carlos said to his blond buddy in a fiendish sounding tone of voice, the palm of his hand moving over the boner I had popped in my uniform trousers.

"H-hey, c-c'mon now, *th-this shit has gone far enough!!*" I seethed miserably as Carlos pulled down my zipper and brazenly reached into my pants.

"Holy fucking shit Carlos, what are you doing with Offisair's cock and balls?" Dennis chortled, gave one of my man tits a mean suck and watched as his buddy reached in past my white under shorts.

"Arrrrrrrhhhhh God!!!!" I seethed, as he didn't handle me all that gently as he brought out my big pride and joy.

I was still up on my tiptoes and squirming and dancing erotically as the two thugs held me tightly by the ass cheeks, Carlos' other hand getting my big eight to nine inches and egg sized juicy balls situated for their perverse pleasures. As much as I hate to admit to it I was hard as a fucking rock and pulsing like crazy, droplets of pre seed oozing from my wide sexy slit. My hairy and mangy balls hung down good and low, filled to the fucking max with my cop slop, slop that I would soon be relieved of.

"Holy fuck Carlos, I'm straight as that crazy boxer guy is, but hooooly fucking shit, just look at the beef stick on Offisair here, look at that stalk he's got!" Dennis said merrily and gave one of my cop tits a mean pinch, twisting the bejesus out of it.

"Ohhhhhhhhrrrr fuck, *fuck it all you bastards,*" I was seething at that point. "You two mugs will pay for this!"

"Come on Dennis, lets see if we can't get our friendly neighborhood offisair here off a few times in between eating his tits for dinner," Carlos said meanly. "I think that wall will be a good landing base for his pig sperm."

"Oh no, no, *fuck no,* you two have got to be joking now!!" I grunted as they moved me closer to the red bricked wall, my cock wagging hard in front of me on total display, the two young men moving me along by squeezing my ass cheeks tighter, practically hoisting me up off the ground.

The thought of these two jokers jacking me off didn't sit well with me let me tell you. Fuck, the thought of any damned mug jacking me off didn't sit well with me. As I was moved closer to the wall I turned my head and looked longingly over at my gun and utility belt on the ground, totally out of my reach.

"Forget about it Offisair," Dennis said meanly and squeezed my behind hard. "A pussy doesn't need a gun. And believe me; *you are going to be our pussy boy tonight.*"

"Okay Dennis, here's the deal," Carlos laughed, grabbing my hard-on in his hand and pointing my big guy at the wall a few feet in front of us. "We'll take turns stroking his big pig crank *and* whoever has him in hand when he pops his nut gets to kiss him, all slurpy and sloppy right on the lips!"

I gulped hard and miserably. This was starting to feel like some kind of twisted love story…

"That should really turn Offisair here on," Carlos said and began stroking me. "Because once you've been kissed by me, you've really been fucking kissed!"

"Fucking bastards, I don't feel like being kissed by two faggot kidnappers like you," I seethed at them.

The two thugs laughed uproariously, leaned down, slurped at my man tits and took turns stroking me and stroking me.

"Oh God no, no, th-this really is too much now," I panted, knowing too well that I was going to cum like gangbusters, knowing that I was going to shoot a load big enough to choke a goddamned horse. "Gods, *fuckers, cop-nappers!*"

Visions of Linda, my present girlfriend passed before my eyes in my mind as the two thugs did their dirty work. She loved stroking and playing with my manhood before having my big cop cock inside her. She called my big cock her big guy and she always said how my big man tits were the control knobs for my big cock. One good squeeze on my man tits always gets me hard and throbbing Linda says. My big sweaty and hairy balls crashed against the front of my uniform trousers as the thugs stroked me a little faster each time they took me in hand anew. They ate and ate my man tits with real and utter gusto, the feeling of their tongue tips on the tips of my nubs driving me totally batty.

"Ohhhhhhhrrrrrr geez, this is a shitty ass thing you guys," I grunted and then spewed a long rope of thick and creamy cop slop. "Ohhhhhhhhhrrrrr got me shootin' my damned load!!"

Looking down I saw that it was Carlos who presently had me in hand. I then looked straight ahead and saw my jazz running down the red brick wall. Fuck, what a sick thing man, two sick things actually, my cop cock in a thug's hand and my jazz on the brick wall of an abandoned apartment building, *fuck, and fuck!!* As Carlos stroked me and Dennis ate one of my man tits I shot another good-sized rope of cop slop and then another and another, grunting and groaning breathlessly.

"Man oh fucking man, just look at Offisair shoot that load," Carlos chortled happily.

When I thought I was done Dennis reached down and gave my big balls a squeeze as Carlos stroked me some more.

"Arrrrrrhhhhhh shhhiiittt," I croaked and another good sized blast of cum erupted from my slit, landing on the wall with the rest of my sexy mess. "Goddamn it all!!!"

I stood there with my head hanging down, humiliation overwhelming me as the two men slurped heartily and meanly on my man tits.

"Ohhhhhrrrrr, shit, that hurts!" I seethed.

"Yeah, sure as shit it does at that Offisair," Carlos said, squeezing the back of my big neck and moving his face close to mine. "Seems that whenever a guy shoots a good sized load of nut juice his whole body becomes super sensitive to the touch, and his tits seem to suffer the most of all."

As he spoke his lips were grazing mine and Dennis was still eating one of my man tits, gobbling at it actually, sending shockwaves of chills and pain through my very being.

"Now c'mon Offisair, give Carlos a big kiss for jacking you the fuck off," Carlos said and brazenly slid his tongue between my quivering lips.

Shocking to me I found myself responding to the guy's sloppy kiss. I sucked his tongue into my mouth and we kissed the fuck out of each other real roughly. His hand caressed the back of my big bull-sized neck as I lowered myself to my feet. Dennis stopped (temporarily) eating my tit to watch Carlos and I kiss.

"Shit, look at that," Dennis quipped. "Fucking cop is really starting to enjoy all this shit. I hope I have you in hand the next time we make you cum Offisair."

When Carlos stopped kissing me a few moments later the two thugs moved me back away from the wall, affording me a good view of my mess as it dripped down the red bricks. They didn't waste any time however and quickly resumed eating my man tits…

"Ohhhhhhhrrrr shhhiiiitttt," I seethed anew. "Come on you perverts, you've had your fun with me. I've fulfilled your goddamned captive cop fantasy! Let me go already!"

But alas, that was not to be. Fuck it all, I had no clue just how much they had in mind for me that night. I stared straight ahead at my mess of cop slop on the wall and to my dismay found myself growing hard and erect again. That was what Linda loved most of all about me that I could shoot my load and with the right coaxing I was soon ready to go again. *But fuck, these guys were not Linda.* My balls hung all sweaty, succulent and filled again with my cop juices as the two thugs ate dinner, namely my poor tits…

It was about fifteen or so minutes later (by my best estimates) when they moved me close to the wall for the second time. Eating my man tits like crazy they again took turns stroking my cop crank. I panted miserably, swearing all sorts of revenge at them, telling them how they would spend the next ten years in jail for assaulting a police officer, but god I have to admit, them eating my tits and stroking my goddamned meat stick was sending chills and thrills through me that were indescribable. Then, all my words and threats were cut short and it was Dennis who had me in hand this time when I popped my load.

"Ohhhhhhhrrrrr fffuuuuccckkkk, fuck, got me creaming like a madman again," I ranted and squirmed up on my toes as Dennis stroked and stroked my sexy mess out of me, the second one.

"Heh, you'll be a madman by the time this night is over Offisair," Dennis laughed as Carlos did the honors of eating one of my man tits as I came and came like crazy, spewing my mess all over the red brick wall for the second goddamned time. "Looks like it's me who gets to kiss that puss of yours this time."

"Fuck you man, fuck you," I garbled breathlessly.

The second I was done spewing my gushy and creamy mess I turned and faced Dennis. Without a word we clamped our mouths down on each others and kissed hard and mean as Carlos went on and fucking on eating one of my tits. My head spun and the erotic pain filled me as it sure as shit drove me crazy to be having one of my tits worked over after just spewing my mess. Dennis slobbered in my mouth, sucked my lips and kissed me like he'd never kissed anyone before. When the thug finally stopped kissing me the two men moved me back from the wall and they both again ate and ate my poor aching man tits.

Now, still trapped in that alley a good hour or so later I was being jacked off for the third fucking time. I stared miserably straight ahead at my dried up cop slop on the wall as the two thugs took turns stroking my big meat, both of them hoping to have me in hand when I shot my load, hoping for a good wet sloppy kiss from Offisair Mach.

"Ohhhhhhhrrrrrr gods you guys," I grunted. "Wh-when is this going to stop? When are you going to let me out of here?"

In response the two thugs laughed hard and it was Dennis who had me in hand when I shot that third load of cop's soup.

"Ohhhhhhhrrrrrr fuck it all!!" I groaned and danced stupidly on my toes as I came and came again.

It had taken a little longer this time, but eventually the thugs stroked me off, lucky Dennis having earned his second kiss. This time the blond thug didn't wait till I was done jazzing. He simply leaned in, planted his lips on mine and we kissed long, hard and crazily. When I was done jazzing for the third time and Dennis had stopped kissing me for the second time the sounds of crooning and slurping again filled the alley as the two thugs moved me again back from the wall, their mouths never leaving my man tits for long at all… I was in a state of hyped up tension and over-sensitivity let me tell you bud. Being stroked off repeatedly and kissed the way I was being kissed was driving me over the edge…

"Mmmmmm, mmmmmmmm…" the two thugs crooned happily and with satisfaction as they ate and ate and ate my man tits.

I had no goddamned choice but to stand there helplessly as they ate my tits, moved their mangy hands over my muscular cop body and squeezed the fuck out of my ass cheeks. It was what was coming next that the bastards would have to gag me for…

When they stopped eating my cop tits to come up for air my poor nubs were swollen to the size of two pointy bullets on my big muscular chest. They were tingling, numb, sore and alive somehow, begging for more attention, yet dreading anymore at the same time. Saliva dripped down my chest from my overworked nipples and to my stomach area as my cock hung semi hard and all slimy between my legs.

"You know Dennis, I'm thinking about how fucking generous we've been to Offisair Mach here, what with getting the pig off three times and really getting him all worked up by eating his big titties," Carlos said, holding tight to one of my sexy ass cheeks.

"What's your point Carlos?" Dennis asked, sounding as if he already knew just what the fuck Carlos was talking about.

"My point, buddy of mine, is that now I'm feeling just a tad bit more than horny," Carlos said meanly, rubbing the boner he was sporting in his jeans. "And I'm really fucking ready to shoot a load or a few myself. Sucking Offisair's tits, making him cum and kissing him sure has my big Puerto Rican cock aching for some attention.

"I hear you bud," Dennis said. "And I think I know full well just what kind of attention that cock of yours wants."

The two thugs looked at me lecherously and menacingly…

"Oh fuck, oh no, you guys wouldn't," I pleaded desperately.

"Let's get 'em lubed up Offisair, because they're going to be taking a trip up your chocolate highway," Carlos said meanly, he and Dennis letting go of my ass cheeks.

Carlos punched me a good hard one right square in the center of my gut.

"HOOFFFFFF!!!" I grunted, taken totally by surprise. "G-God, that's awful man, to gut punch a guy when he has no damned defenses…"

Smiling Dennis followed suit, giving me a good one right in the same spot that Carlos just had.

"HOOOFFFF!!!!" I grunted again and leaned my shoulders down, trying to take what they were dishing out on me. "HOOOFFFF!!!!!!!!" (Another gut punch from Carlos.)

They gut punched me over and over, moving me back toward the wall where they had made me shoot my load. Then, horror of horrors, when I was standing real close to the wall Carlos grabbed a handful of my cock and swung it forward, mashing it against the brick wall.

"OHHHHRRRRRRRR!!!!" I cried out pitifully and shook like a leaf as they then turned me around with my back against the wall.

When my back was pressed against the wall I could feel the remnants of my jazz slithering all over me back there. My poor cock felt awful after having been mashed against the brick wall. The two thugs gut punched me a few more times each for good measure, really causing the wind to be knocked out of me. Thankfully though this time I only dribbled saliva from my mouth, no blood appeared this time. I heaved and gasped against the wall, not realizing that the two thugs were working on getting my uniform pants off me over my shoes and socks. When I was wearing just my white sweat soaked and piss stained under shorts (with my cock and balls dangling out of them) my black rubber soled shoes and navy blue cotton socks the two thugs each gave me one more hard, really hard gut punch each, sending me plummeting to my knees. All I could do was heave, gasp, grunt, and pray for one good breath. Saliva foamed around my trembling lips as I looked up helplessly at my two captors. God almighty, what a horrible word for a cop to call two guys, *his captors*... Admittedly at this point I was beyond terrified and thinking that they were going to kill me for sure.

"Keep that mouth filled with your cop spit Offisair," Carlos said, pulling the zipper down on his jeans. "You're going to need it to get my big Puerto Rican cock good and fucking slick."

"Yeah, that way it won't hurt so much when we fuck your goddamned shit hole!" Dennis quipped, taking down his jeans zipper as well. "Like I said Offisair, *you are our pussy tonight!*"

"N-no, I-I won-won't," I garbled softly as Carlos dangled one of the biggest, fattest and meanest looking one-eyed monsters in my face.

His cock was of the jumbo sized that was for sure, along with two big fat goose egg sized balls in a hairy stinking brown sac.

"Oh you will, *you'll do this and lots more Offisair*," Carlos teased me meanly, rubbing his piss slit against my trembling lips. "Now, open fucking wide and if I feel teeth once you are going to be the sorriest offisair in the whole goddamned city."

I actually was already the sorriest officer in the city. Choking back tears of utter humiliation I did as I was told and Carlos slid his stinking manhood into my mouth. I closed my lips around it, drooled my saliva all over it and began sucking as he thrust in deeper, brought his cock slightly out and thrust back in again.

"Ohhhhhrrrr yeah, ooooooo fuck Dennis, this cop's mouth is like velvet, real fucking sweet," Carlos mused, running the palm of a hand over my buzz-cut head, tugging slightly on my short hairs.

"Mmmmmfffff..." I sputtered around the big cock invading my mouth, slowly being thrust deeper and deeper toward my throat.

Carlos' cock literally filled my craw, cutting off my breathing. And to put it plainly his cock tasted awful, as if he hadn't washed for a few days. The taste of sweat mixed with sour and rancid piss wafted over my taste buds and slid down my throat. Then, Carlos' jeans crotch was against my face and I saw his dark curly pubic hairs in front of me. He held me by the back of my neck as he viciously face fucked me and fucked my throat.

"Oh yeah, get my cock good and slick you hot stud cop," Carlos grunted, force feeding me his cock.

He slowly slid the huge thing out of my throat, rested it on my tongue and gave me a few seconds to breathe before plowing it back down my throat again. I looked up at the guy, my mouth and throat filled with his cock and looked at him with eyes filled with anger, hatred and total humiliation…yet my cock was hard as a fucking rock between my legs. *Gawd!!*

"Fuck man, I am getting close already Offisair!" Carlos grunted. "Goddamn it Pig, I am going to feed you one of the best and biggest loads of jazz in the whole fucking city!!"

He positioned his cock halfway in my mouth, held it in place and said one word to me, "Suck!" Without much choice in the matter I did as I was told and as I sucked and sucked Carlos spewed a load that seemed to equal all three of the ones that he and Dennis had squeezed and stroked out of me.

"Ohhhhhrrrrr yeah, fucking Offisair Mach really knows how to suck a cock Dennis," Carlos gasped loudly, holding me by the back of the neck as he force-fed me his slimy juices.

"Can't wait to find out for myself," Dennis chortled, standing by with his big Irish-sized sausage like cock in his hand.

"I'm almost done here bud," Carlos grunted throatily. "Just a little more, and then after this we'll fuck his shit hole till all he has left back there will be a slimy and messy pussy hole. OHHHHRRRRRR yeah, fucking A Offisair!!!"

As I sucked him I gained a good rhythm and was able to gulp down his messy sticky juices as he filled and refilled my craw with it.

"Arrrrrhhhhhh fuckkkk, better than the way my old lady sucks me Cop!!" Carlos chuckled sadistically. "Real sweet mouth you got there…"

When he was done he once more jammed his cock in my throat, grabbed me meanly by the sides of my face and pissed, *fuck, the bastard used my throat as a damned urinal.*

"RRRRFFFFFFF!!!" I wailed as his hot yellow and rancid stream filled my gullet.

"Now that is downright awful man," Dennis laughed. "Nothing is worse for a cop than having some guy pissing in his mouth. Tsk, tsk, that's no way to treat an offisair of the law Carlos…"

The two men laughed heartily and Carlos' cock emerged from my mouth all slimy and semi hard. I knew the thug would have no problem whatsoever getting hard all over again when the time came to fuck my damned shit hole, as he so aptly phrased it. Without missing a beat and without letting me catch my breath Dennis then slid his big meat pole into my mouth…

"Mmmmffff…" I sputtered angrily and drooled all over the other thug's rancid tasting cock.

"Oh yeah, just as you said Carlos, like velvet his mouth is," Dennis panted, taking me by the back of the neck as he, like Carlos, slid his cock further toward my throat with each thrust.

Dennis' cock was not as long as Carlos' was, but it sure was fat, a real Irish sausage sized cock Dennis had. My jaws ached as I tried to open wider to accommodate him. I squeezed my eyes shut as he thrust meanly in and out and in and out of my mouth, forcing me to suck him, his smelly balls crashing against the bottom of my chin…

"Come on Offisair, suck my meat, get ready to swallow another good mess of creamy sperm," Dennis said commandingly, his cock skewering my mouth and jamming in and out of my throat.

He forced me to lick his piss hole with the tip of my tongue. It killed me inside that all I could do was kneel there and do as I was being told. His piss hole tasted just like that, piss. He made me eat the droplets of pre cum that oozed from his slit and then he slowly filled my mouth again with his meat. Fuck, I was a cop, a New York City police officer. I was supposed to prevent things like this from happening to people. Now look, I was being raped and used as a goddamned sex toy of sorts.

"Ohhhhhrrrr yeah, I-I'm ready Carlos," Dennis grunted madly. "I'm goin' to cum like never before in my damned life!! Ohhhhhhhhrrrr fucking A, this stud cop is making me crazy the way he sucks cock."

As Dennis' creamy hot load filled my mouth I leaned my head back and gulped it down as fast as I could. It was vile and rancid, but as I said, I had no fucking choice in the matter.

"If you need to piss, just use his throat like I did," Carlos said to his buddy, giving Dennis' ass a squeeze. "Fucking cop may not admit it yet, but he loves the taste of piss."

The two men laughed meanly and heartily. And sure enough, when Dennis was done he, like Carlos, jammed his big tool down my throat and pissed. He held me by the ears, squeezing them tight and painfully as he filled my gullet with his rancid yellow stream.

"RRRFFFFFFFF!!!!!" I gurgled, practically choking on his mess.

"Ha, bet you never thought in all your worst fears something like this happening to you eh Offisair?" Carlos asked me, grinning down at me from ear to ear.

All I could do in response was look up at him blankly as I drank down the last of Dennis' piss…

A few minutes later I was sitting on the ground against a garbage pail while Carlos and Dennis stood over me taking a cigarette break. My legs were spread and my mouth was awful with the taste of cum and piss. I was catching my breath as the two thugs stood over me, flicking cigarette ashes on me.

"Fucking best idea you ever had Dennis my man, to pose as a homeless guy in this alley so that some unwitting cop pig would wander in," Carlos said, patting his buddy on the shoulder.

"I know, some of my buddies in upstate New York did it one time to a trooper there," Dennis said after puffing his cigarette and flicking the ashes down on me. "Ever since then, that trooper comes to them for a daily shit hole fucking."

"We'll just see if that's the case with you two bastards!" I yelled up at my two captors, their cocks dangling out of their jeans along with their mangy and stinking balls. "I swear to God and all his angels in Heaven I will see you two locked up for this shit!!! I ain't some pussy upstate trooper you low life scumbags!!!!"

"Come on Offisair, lick my balls," Carlos said, pulling me up to my knees by my upper arm.

Without question I leaned forward and sucked one of Carlos' big balls into my mouth. I licked, sucked and kissed it too.

"There we go," Carlos panted. "That'll keep him quiet while we enjoy our cigarette break."

The two men looked down at me with total satisfaction as I serviced Carlos' damned nuts…

When they finished their cigarettes Dennis pushed three garbage cans together in the shape of a triangle. I just kept right on licking and slathering Carlo's stinking balls.

"Oh yeah, fucking Offisair Mach just loves my big balls," Carlos said breathlessly, holding his big hard cock in hand. "And you're going to love having my big cock plow that shit chute of yours in a few minutes."

When Carlos hauled me to my feet I saw that Dennis had placed the three garbage pails in the perfect position for lying someone across, namely a trapped cop who was now feeling a fear like none ever before.

"Oh God no, no, *please you guys,*" I pleaded as the two men hauled me up off the ground by my upper arms and socked ankles in a laying down position, my face looking down at the ground. "P-put me the fuck down you bastards! This is more than a shitty thing to be doing to a cop!!"

"We'll have to get these cute under shorts of his off him Dennis," Carlos said as they positioned me on my stomach atop the smelly turned over garbage cans, my sexy butt positioned just where the fuck they wanted it.

My butt was up in the air and a ready target for just what the hell they had in mind. Carlos did the honors of tearing the back of my under shorts off me and cramming them in my mouth.

"You'll need to be gagged for this Offisair," Carlos said as I garbled and protested around my underpants being crammed in my mouth.

"GGGRRRHHHHMMMFFFF!!!" I ranted angrily.

Fuck, but when I had gotten dressed that morning the last place that I thought I would find my (torn) under shorts was in my mouth, being used as a makeshift gag of sorts. They spread my legs good and fucking wide, exposing my funky virgin butt hole.

"Oh man, oh fucking man, nice tight looking shit hole you got back here Offisair Mach," Carlos said, prodding two fingers deep into my anal canal.

"RRRmmmmmmffffff!!!" I gasped and lifted my upper body up off the garbage pails.

The two men laughed and then Carlos took position between my spread legs, pressing the tip of his big cock against the walls of my poor hole.

"MMMMFFFFF!!!" I gasped, looking back at him and pleadingly shaking my head "no" from side to side.

Smiling devilishly, Carlos grabbed my socked ankles, lifted my legs and slowly slid his huge manhood into me.

"Ohhhhrrrrr yeah, fucking tight shit chute he has," Carlos panted, looking down at me as his cock disappeared inside me.

"Only for now Carlos," Dennis laughed. "After we get done with him he's going to be stretched good and wide back there."

"HA, so fucking true," Carlos chortled, my feet held tight next to his face as he thrust in and out of my hole.

He sniffed the sides of my damned socks as he did his goddamned dirty work, namely sliding and plowing deeper and deeper into my damned bung hole, filling me, stretching me back there and torturing the bejesus out of me with his manhood, spearing me with it.

"RRRRMMMFFFFFF!!!!" I railed wildly, the tatters of my under shorts hanging embarrassingly out of my mouth.

When Carlos was fully inside me I swear I thought his cock would slide out of my mouth, that's how goddamned deep he was in me. He thrust out a little bit only to plow me deeper upon reentry. He licked my shoes and sniffed my socks as he held my feet aloft, deep fucking me like crazy. My head spun away and then after a while I heard Carlos exclaiming that he was going to shoot his load.

"Ohhhhrrr yeah, fucking best piece of ass I've had in more than a while you hot offisair!" Carlos panted and then I felt his hot juices flooding my hole. "Yeah, real nice shit chute you got there Cop!"

He thrust in and out like crazy as he filled me and filled me with his juices, holding tight to my ankles, keeping my legs aloft and in pain.

I didn't even notice when Carlos' cock was out of my hole and Dennis' took its place. All I knew a few seconds later was that Carlos was standing over me and Dennis was holding my feet aloft and fucking the tar out of me.

"Feeling good Offisair?" Carlos asked me snidely and patted me on the head.

"RRRRRMMMMFFFFFF!!!" I sputtered angrily up at him.

My cock hung semi hard between the garbage cans I was slung across. As Dennis fucked me, and fucked me, I pissed long and hard on the ground. The two thugs fucking me like a cheap whore made me have to piss like crazy, not to mention that they hadn't let me piss after having shot my load those three times earlier. Like most guys I have to piss like crazy after I've popped a good nut. I felt Dennis' big Irish balls crashing against my ass cheeks when he announced that he was about to spew his load inside me.

"Ohhhhhhrrr yeah, I am cumming now Offisair!!" Dennis panted, holding tight to my ankles, his cock jammed deep inside me. "Oh fucking A, going to fill your cop's shit hole with my hot love juices!! Fucking stud cop taking my cock and cum, fucking A and B man!!!!"

I squeezed my eyes shut as Dennis filled my hole with his hot and sticky mess. My poor anal canal felt as if it had been stretched already beyond its limits as Dennis' pound of beef was wedged tightly in there. He thrust in and out of me as he seemed to cum and cum and cum and when he was done his cock slipped out of my hole and a mess of cum dripped from me back there, humiliating!

"Oh yeah, he's all nice and moist back there now Dennis," Carlos said sadistically and happily, heaving me up off the garbage cans and up into his big arms like a bridegroom lifting his new wife. "*Now he's really our pussy.*"

Strong fucker the guy had to be to be holding me aloft like that in his arms. I'm no fucking lightweight after all. Carlos smiled wickedly at me; asked me if I was ready for some more and kissed me hard on my gagged mouth. He spun around a few times with me still in his arms, teasing me, mocking me and then he laid me down on my back across the garbage cans, grabbed my socked ankles and slammed his huge cock again into my waiting and gaping hole.

"RRRRRmmmffffff!!!" I wailed in misery, looking upwards at the sky with my eyes squeezed halfway shut as the bastard plowed me again, thrusting harder and harder with each shove inside me.

For whatever the fuck the reason it hurt more while I was on my back as the thug speared me. I guess the position one is in plays a mean part in just how it'll feel when you're getting fucked. He then let go of my ankles, rested my feet on his shoulders and rammed and rammed still further into me. By now we were both sweating, he in ecstasy and me in outright fucking total misery. I felt as if my whole life had come down to this horrible moment. As Carlos fucked me harder and harder and totally savagely I glanced to my side and saw that Dennis was again hard and throbbing, his cock in hand, ready and waiting to plow me again as well. My tears flowed from the sides of my eyes and then Carlos shot another good and hefty load of thug spunk into my hole, filling me yet again with his juices.

"Ohhhhhrrrrr yeah, you fucking hot cop," Carlos grunted and gave my sexy ass a good hard slap as he slid out of me, lowering my legs as he went.

I felt his cum dripping from my hole…

I lay there with my muscular legs dangling off the garbage pails as Dennis took position in front of me. I whimpered miserably as he hoisted my legs up and plowed into me with real gusto…

"RRRRMMMFFFF!!!!" I wailed as my hole was invaded again.

By the time it was over they had both fucked me one more time each. My hole was sopping wet with their mangy juices, my legs were aching and I was sweating and stinking with it like crazy…

They propped me against the wall where I had shot my loads earlier and took a few final sucks and slurps at my wrecked man tits. My torn under shorts were out of my mouth, what was left of them still embarrassingly around my waist, my cock and balls hanging out of them. Obviously they couldn't fuck me anymore. They had to be sore as all hell to put it plainly.

"Ohhhhhrrrrrr, f-fuckers, bastards, y-you guys are so under arrest," I whimpered miserably, sounding like a cop in brutal pain.

"Really Offisair?" Carlos chuckled, holding up the key to my handcuffs. "You'll have to get yourself in order, get dressed and then catch us if you want to arrest us you fucking stud cop."

He unlocked the handcuffs, but before I could do shit Dennis gut punched me good and fucking hard, sending me sprawling to the ground.

"HHHOOFFFFF!!!" I grunted and slid to the ground.

As I heaved and heaved for breath one of them undid the ropes around my upper arms…

When I looked up I saw them walking quickly out of the alley. I slowly got to my knees and crawled in total pain over to where my uniform was on the ground. I grabbed my radio and was about to click it on. Was I really going to tell headquarters what had just happened to me? Fuck it all!!!! What a fucked up and twisted situation this was.

Raped like crazy, brutally beaten, used like a sex toy and not able to report it. I bit down on my lower lip and clicked off the radio. With my hands shaking I slowly got my uniform back on. Standing was not easy due to the pain in my poor gut and in my legs and worst of all in my shit hole. I choked on my tears as I buttoned up my shirt. It irritated the fuck out of my wrecked tits and unbelievable to me, my cock grew hard in my uniform pants. Before exiting the alley behind the apartment building I took my manhood out of my pants and jacked myself off twice more, spewing my load all over that wall where I had shot my load three times earlier. I picked up my utility belt, snapped it back around my waist and slowly exited the alley, the awful scene of my capture and rape. I have never seen Carlos and Dennis since.

In the Woods

When my buddy and I met Hector we had found him in the woods and not under ordinary circumstances mind you. He wasn't hunting or playing a friendly game of War with his buddies; rather, the handsome bulky muscle boy was strung up by his wrists from a tree branch, and gagged. A white cloth was tied and crammed tightly over his mouth, his lips jutting out and under it. Now, most people upon finding something so bizarre and unusual, finding someone in that kind of position would have immediately cut him down, but not us. The way the muscle boy was hanging there totally naked except for a filthy pair of white sweat socks on his feet, sweating profusely, and sort of beat-up looking drove us wild on sight.

"Holy fuck man, look at that," I said to Ronald and pointed as we made our way toward the dangling and spectacularly handsome muscle boy. "I cannot believe what the fuck I'm seeing."

"Hey man, maybe he's dead," Ronald said to me, an air of caution in his voice.

"Nah, his big chest is moving up and down, he's breathing," I said as we walked slowly and cautiously over to where the big lug was hanging.

When he heard the crackle of leaves under our feet as we approached he looked up and saw us. The sight of his handsome face beguiled me in an instant. He had short cut cropped black hair, marble black eyes, and a look of terror on his handsome face that stole my heart away on sight. As I said he was a bulky looking muscle boy and all pumped up, yet chunky in certain spots, like his thighs and ass for instance. As Ronald and I approached him with our backpacks in hand a look of hope mixed with dread filled the guy's handsome face. The muscles in his long and lanky triceps and bowling ball sized biceps flexed involuntarily as he squirmed in the bondage. I guessed his age to be anywhere in the early to mid twenties. His body was completely hairless, smooth, save for the hair on his head, the thick bushes of hair in his armpits, and his thick black sexy pubic bush. His skin was an olive complexion with two dark brown silver dollar sized nipples on his big barrel-sized muscular chest, real chewy looking those nipples of his were let me tell you. His cock was softly dangling between his legs and his balls were the size of two small ripe plums, hanging there in a real juicy looking sac. From the way he was sweating I guessed he had been out there for a while at that point. But oh man, his arms stretched tightly above him really were a mess of muscles upon muscles. It really made me wonder how a muscle headed guy like this could possibly have wound up in a position like the one he was in.

"Mmmmmmmmmffff…" he muttered as Ronald and I set our backpacks down in front of him.

"Hey Big boy," I said to him. "Now how the hell did you wind up in a position like this?"

"MMMMFFFF…" he said again, a little louder this time, a look in his eyes saying he thought we were stupid for expecting him to reply while gagged.

Ronald and I stood at his sides, looking him over hungrily. He was scented and real sexily musty with the odor of his muscle boy sweat. I took the gag out of his mouth, leaving it dangling around his big bull sized neck. I somehow had the feeling that we would need to gag him again.

"Oh man, thanks," he said in a deep guttural sounding voice and licked his dried lips a few times. "Thanks man, oh fuck, I sure am glad to see you guys. Actually, I'm fucking glad to see anybody other than those two bastards who put me out here. I'll fucking kill those two when I get my hands on them!"

"Which bastards are those?" Ronald asked looking around nervously as the afternoon sun beat down on us, cooking the muscle boy in all his musculature and nakedness.

"My two so called buddies who left me out here after sucking the fuck out of my poor cock and making it feel real sore," the strung-up muscle boy said angrily. "Some fucked up friends they turned out to be. Fuckers sucked me till my poor cock was fucking sore and my balls were drained of my spunk, then those fuckers sucked me some more. Made me shoot goddamned dry loads, man oh fucking man, that shit can drive a poor guy crazy!"

"Your two buddies sucked you off till you were bone dry?" I asked the muscle boy, getting a good hearty whiff of his hairy armpit as I stepped closer to him, looking at his soft but plump cock resting over his big juicy balls.

His armpit was just as musty smelling as the rest of him, like a real muscle boy's armpits should smell after he's been worked over for a while.

"Yeah, fucking guys even worked on my tits for a while," he said miserably. "Fucking tortured the poor things till I was screaming so loud they'd *had to* gag me."

"Yeah, now that you mention it these tits of yours do look somewhat sore and chewed up at that," Ronald said and took that as an excuse to squeeze one of the muscle boy's tits real hard.

"YOOWWWWCCHHHH!!! Hey man, that's not funny!!" the handsome muscle boy ranted at Ronald. "I only allowed all this shit because of the game I lost."

"You allowed yourself to be tied up like this?" I asked the guy in total disbelief. "All naked except for your goddamned socks buddy?"

"Yeah, my two work buddies and I are staying at one of those cabins back at the camp grounds," he explained. "We're spending some time off there, just kicking back and relaxing. Fuck, it looks like I didn't get to relax all that much though huh?"

"What are you and your buddies taking some time off from?" Ronald asked the guy and again squeezed one of his sore nipples.

"OWWWWWCCHHHH!!! Hey man, leave my goddamned tits alone already!!" the muscle boy again ranted at my good buddy Ronald. "We're construction workers. We had been working seven days a week straight for more than a month and we finally got some time off. We had gotten a job renovating the seventh floor of an office building. The vice president of the company that hired us wanted the job done fast so we were forced to work seven days a week."

"So you all went on vacation together and they tied you up out here?" I asked the big guy.

"Well, I didn't expect to get tied up, hell, I didn't expect to be made to walk through the woods in just my goddamned socks either, as you called 'em a few minutes ago," he said as he hung there sweating, grunting in between talking to us and stinking like a real fucking stud. "I didn't expect to be sucked off by my two buddies or to have my tits tortured either. Shit, I'm not even gay! I didn't know they were. But when Richard suggested a game of cards with severe consequences for the loser my curiosity was instantly fucking piqued."

"Richard is one of your buddies I take it," Ronald said and rubbed the tip of his thumb over the muscle boy's nipple that he had squeezed twice.

"Yeah, Richard and Bob, they're my work buddies," he went on. "I'm Hector."

I guessed his nationality to be Puerto Rican Spanish.

"I'm Alex," I said. "This is my buddy Ronald."

"It sure is great to meet both of you," Hector said happily, his face lighting up in a beautiful white teethed smile. "I would shake your hands but you'll have to wait till you untie me."

"That's okay Hector, we'll just shake this," Ronald said, grabbed Hectors soft cock real tight and shook it vigorously up and down a few times and then from side to side.

"Yahhhhhhhhh!!! Hey man, *what is your fucking problem?*" Hector seethed in Ronald's face. "First you squeeze my goddamned sore nipples and now you fucking play shake with my goddamned cock! And I cannot believe that you two haven't untied me! Gods, I'm having a goddamned conversation with you two while I'm all tied up and wearing just my stinking socks!!"

When Ronald let go of Hector's cock and I took my turn grabbing it and shaking it the bound up muscle boy looked at us fearfully, a cold and harsh reality setting in.

"Shit, *shit,*" looks like now I'm in even more trouble," Hector said dejectedly.

"What kind of game did you lose that caused you to wind up out here like this?" I asked the guy after letting go of his cock.

Before he replied Ronald treated the poor tied up guy to a good hearty drink of cold water from his canteen. Hector's lips slurped passionately around the top of the canteen as he sipped down the cool and refreshing water.

"Th-thanks guy," Hector said happily and licked his lips. "Well, Richard had suggested an old fashioned game of War. Simple game, first guy to lose all his cards wins. But when we all sat down to play Richard said that he had a great yet scary idea. Bob asked him what the idea was and I was curious as hell too. At first Richard didn't want to tell us, saying that we were probably chicken shit. That was when I started asking him what his idea was. Richard explained that it could be fun for the two winners if they were allowed to do whatever they wanted to the loser, short of maiming or murdering him of course. He said it was a thing that he and his boyhood friends used to do while growing up. He went on to tell us how he'd had some real cool adventures with those friends of his. Well, of course Bob and I sat there mulling it over, and I was the stupid fuck that said let's go for it. I figured I wouldn't lose and I could finally get back at Richard for all the jokes he had played on me on the job."

"What kind of jokes?" Ronald asked and took one of the muscle boy's nipples between his thumb and first two fingers. "And don't tell me to let go of this tit of yours guy, you're in no position to do any fucking thing except what you're told!"

"Shit!!" Hector grunted breathlessly as Ronald teased and twirled his nipple in his fingers. "Well, yeah, jokes that Richard played on me. Okay, one time he got a hold of my lunch sandwich and poured a heaping amount of hot sauce on it, knowing that I usually gulped my sandwiches down in two big bites. Fuck man, I was shitting my brains out all day that time. In and out of the crapper, what a fucked up day that was. Another time the fucking guy put cement glue on the bottoms of my work boots while I was hunkered down and working on the bottom portion of a wall. When I stood up and found myself stuck to the floor my two buddies had a grand old time laughing at me. While I stood there trying to pull my feet off the floor they whipped my ass with their leather belts. Seems like they're always looking for excuses to do that. Fuck, I had to take my boots off and slice them off the floor. Ruined a good pair of boots that time. Richard offered to pay for the boots but I played the part of a good sport and refused the offer. The worst thing he ever did was slip an ex-lax in my chocolate milk while we were having lunch."

"Ha, you're kind of a big booted guy for chocolate milk Muscle boy, but I'll bet you shit your guts out that time, ha, bet you were in the crapper all the live long day," Ronald said laughingly and went on squeezing and teasing the guy's nipple.

"Yeah, worse than the time with the hot sauce," Hector said miserably and looked at us pleadingly. "L-look guys, are you two going to cut me down or what? My arms are aching like you would not fucking believe and I'm sweating and stinking like a pig, *and* I really want to get back to the cabin. Not to mention the facts that those shit for brains friends of mine beat on me and I have insect bights all over me. I really could use some calamine lotion right about now. *Fuck, I want to teach Richard a lesson before the day is out.*"

"We'll consider it, after you tell us about the infamous card game you lost at," Ronald said and squeezed Hector's poor nipple super-hard, getting a real loud scream of pain out of the muscle boy. "And then tell us what your two buddies did to you before leaving you tied up out here."

"Oh man Ronald, you are a sadistic bastard," I said teasingly and squatted in front of the strung up Hector. "This poor kid is sweating in his goddamned socks and you're going to make him tell a story… HA!!!"

I sniffed the muscle boy's balls and cock. They smelled and reeked of sweat, saliva and man scent. A wicked smile played across my lips. Hector was not going to be returning to his cabin and his buddies for a while, *not for quite a while yet.* With no other choice than to do as he was told he went on to tell the story of the card game.

"Richard shuffled the cards and dealt them between Bob, him, and I, face down of course," Hector said, beginning the story. "We were all comfortably dressed in jeans, tee shirts, and our work boots, sitting around the table in the kitchen area of the cabin. When the game started it looked like I was in the lead to winning, I won the first three hands easily. I teased Richard about how I was going to whip his ass. I was going to totally teach him a lesson for all the fucked up jokes he had played on me. He just smiled and said it ain't over till it's over.

Well, halfway into the game I was down to less than half my cards and to be perfectly frank I was shaking in my goddamned boots. Lady luck had really turned her back on me it seemed. At two points in the game we had all thrown down matching number cards. And I ask you guys, what the fuck are the chances of that???

I lost both wars, which is eight cards lost and then I lost the next few hands. When it was pretty obvious that I didn't stand a snowball's chance in hell of winning Richard snidely asked me what I had meant earlier about whipping his ass. Bob happily said that once my last card was gone that they would be whipping *my* ass, literally. As I said, some buddies I have. Well, I lost the game, obviously. I threw down my last card, lost the round, and sat there in my chair, looking miserably at my two buddies, regretting that I had agreed to Richard's idea for the loser. They didn't waste any time those two buddies of mine. Richard ordered me to strip down to my sweat socks as he and Bob got to their feet. I looked up at them in disbelief. Strip down???

What was up with that shit? I told Richard that I had had no idea that the loser would have to take his clothes off. Richard leaned over me and quickly reminded me that the loser had to do *every fucking thing* that the winners said, and gave me a hard pat on the face. I grudgingly got to my feet and stripped down to my white sweat socks, pushing them down to my ankles. I stood there naked as a fucking jaybird before my two buddies.

Now let me tell you guys, its one thing to be naked in front of strangers in a locker room at the gym because nobody is really checking you out. But in this case I was naked except for my stinking socks in front of two of my best buddies in the whole world and *there is* something real humiliating about that let me tell you. They both snickered meanly at the fact that my tube steak was hard, thick and pulsing between my legs. Fuck man, my poor cock was fear hard. Believe me; I was not turned on by what was happening at that moment. I knew Richard's sadistic side and I knew that I was in for nothing good.

Bob asked Richard what he wanted to do to me first. Richard said he would tell him while I was in the bathroom. Richard ordered me to go and piss, shit, drink some water, say some prayers, whatever, adding that once they began I would not be permitted those luxuries anymore. With a look of defeat on my face I went into the bathroom. I pissed what I could into the bowl from my hard tube steak. I didn't have to shit. I did say a few quick prayers though. I gulped down a few glasses of cold water and then, a few minutes later exited the bathroom. My two buddies were now standing there, each of them holding a good length of rope in their hands. When Richard saw the quizzical look on my face he quickly explained that they were going to have to tie me up to get the fun started. I felt miserable as I walked over to them, my cock now only semi hard and wagging between my legs. Richard next ordered me to cross my arms up behind me.

"Why didn't you just tell them to go fuck themselves?" Ronald asked Hector as he now teased the fuck out of both the muscle boy's sore nipples. "I mean, much as I love my buddy Alex here it'll be a cold day in hell before I let him rope me the fuck up. Fucking guy is the worst practical joker in the world."

"Thank you for that compliment Ronald," I said as I squatted there stealing licks at the bound up muscle boy's sweaty and stinky balls.

"I-I wanted to be a good sport about it, I wanted to show them that I would go along with the set rules," Hector went on, gasping and grunting in between words as we teased his nipples and balls.

"And besides Richard and Bob are built like brick shit houses, even bigger than I am. When my arms were securely roped up behind me in three places my two buddies slid their black leather belts off the loops of their jeans. They took a few steps back behind me and began whipping the fuck out of my big ass cheeks, really laying into them hard. I screamed and grunted miserably in pain as my two buddies really whaled into my poor butt cheeks.

I clenched my teeth and tried my best to deal with the stinging pain. It wasn't long before they had me dancing around stupidly in my socks as they continued dealing blow after horrible blow to my ass cheeks. Richard taunted me awfully, saying that I bet I wished that it were him getting his ass whipped instead of me.

I swore like a captured marine and told him that one day I would get my chance. After a while I was sweating and practically in tears as they still went on and on thrashing my ass."

At that point Ronald let go of Muscle boy's nipples and stepped behind him, looking at his ass cheeks, grinning sadistically.

"Hmmm, now that you mention it these big buns of yours do look all red and striped, real beat up looking," Ronald said meanly and jokingly at the same time.

Then, Ronald opened the palms of his hands and grabbed two good handfuls of the over-sized melon shaped globes of the bound muscle boy. He squeezed them liberally, loving the silky feel of them in his big hands.

"Oh man, oh fuck, what a butt this guy has Alex," Ronald said, really squeezing and kneading Hector's globes. "And they're still warm from the beating his two buddies gave them. "Fuck man, *they must have really beaten him hard.*"

I noticed how Hector wasn't saying a word as my buddy Ronald squeezed and delighted in palming the fuck out of his big ass cheeks. Ronald looked as happy as those women in the old Charmin toilet tissue commercials who were always caught by Mr. Whipple when they would be "squeezing the Charmin…"

"Hey Ronald, lets see if we can't get this guy off," I suddenly suggested eagerly, giving Hector's soft cock a few pulls. "After that he can go on with his story."

With that said I brazenly gobbled Hector's soft and sore cock into my mouth and began sucking it, hard.

"Hoooooooo no, oh no," Hector piped up breathlessly as I sucked his cock and Ronald kneaded his butt cheeks.

"Shut the fuck up Muscle boy," Ronald said and gave Hector a good hard and resounding slap on his wounded ass cheeks. "You are in no fucking position to be telling us what we can or can't do to you!"

As I sucked Hector's cock I felt it getting somewhat hard in my mouth. Ronald hunkered down behind him, spread Muscle boy's glorious cheeks apart, and plunged his tongue into the pink and gaping hole.

"Ohhhhhhrrr you fucking bastards," Hector panted in a mixture of ecstasy and misery. "Of all the fucking people to have found me…"

Ronald and I feasted heartily on the strung up muscle headed guy and with real zeal and total gusto. The sounds of slurping and sucking filled the air around us, along with the sounds of Hector's deep breaths and loud grunts. When the muscle boy's cock was hard, pulsing and tingling in my mouth I drove the guy crazy by sucking just the tip of it with my lips. Ronald's tongue was buried deep in the muscle boy's stink hole, holding his glorious ass cheeks spread good and fucking wide. Hector panted miserably, grunted and groaned like a real stud, and stunk of true man sweat. I ran my hands up and down his muscular legs, toyed with his filthy sweat socks, pulling them up and pushing them back down again, and sucked his cock deep into my mouth again.

"Ohhhhhhhrrrr God, goin' to have me shootin' a dry load any second now you fucking fucks!!" Hector seethed and arched his muscular body forward. "Swear to both of you though when I'm untied I'll teach you and those two so called buddies of mine a very much needed lesson!"

"You're going to have to *get* untied first guy," Ronald said tauntingly to him as I sucked the guy like crazy.

"Ohhhhhrrrr man, goin' to cum now you fucking cock sucker!!" Hector panted wildly and in a high pitched tone of voice, looking down at me as I did my dirty work. "oooooooohhhhhh shit, *shit...*"

I took Hector's cock out of my mouth, held it in my fist, and it spurted a small trickle of ball juice. The cum slithered from his piss slit and just stuck there.

"OHHHHHHHHHHHHHHH FUCCCCKKKKKK!!!!!" Hector reeled.

"Looks like you're getting your wet loads back Muscle boy," I said jovially and slurped the small spurt from the tip of his cock. "Maybe if *we* work you over and milk you for a while you'll get a second wind. Hey Ronald, let's eat Muscle head's sore nips. After shooting his load just now I'll bet they're all sensitive and tingling."

Ronald jumped to his feet along side me and together we leaned down over Hector's massive chest. We each slurped one of his exquisite nipples into our mouths, running our hands over his stomach region and his big pecs.

"Ohhhhhhhh god, you fuckers!!!" he groaned miserably as we nursed heartily at his nipples.

I was able to taste the underlying remains of the saliva his two buddies had left on his big nips from earlier. Judging from the way the muscle boy's nipples were so overly erect and sensitive I guessed that his two so called buddies had really delighted in slurping and sucking the very fuck out of them. Well, Ronald and I were going to have our turn at this muscled hunk too. Shit, just looking at the gorgeous dark eyed stud made me want to kidnap him and never let him go. After we'd worked him into a new layer of sweat we stopped slurping his nipples, gave him some water, and ordered him to continue telling us about what his two buddies, Richard and Bob did to him. Hector took a deep breath, looked down at his wrecked nips for a moment and picked up the story at the point where they were still whipping his poor naked ass cheeks with their leather belts.

"After a good fifteen minutes or so of continuous and horrendous raps with the leather belts, I was totally sweating and my ass cheeks felt like they were on fire," Hector said, continuing the story. "Shit, my cheeks felt hot enough to fry a goddamned egg on, but Richard and Bob still didn't stop beating the fuck out of them. They ordered me to bend over the table we had played the game of cards at and to spread my legs as wide as possible. As I walked over to the table they stayed behind me, whacking my ass cheeks some more. At that point I was choking back tears. When I was leaning over the table and my socked feet were just about touching the floor they took position a few feet away from me and went on belting my poor ass cheeks. A few times they whacked the backs of my thighs, getting some real squeals of misery out of me. Fuck man, hurts like the goddamned devil to get the backs of your thighs whipped with a leather belt. My big juicy balls were dangling dangerously between my spread legs. What I feared happened more than once. The belts connected meanly with my balls. I screamed in tortured agony, nearly flying right out of my damned socks. I yelled at them how what a horrible and fucked up thing it was to belt a poor guy's balls, but Richard and Bob ignored me and just continued whacking my ass cheeks over and over and over again."

As Hector related his story my cock was beyond hard in my fatigue style hiking pants. From the bulge that I could see that Ronald was sporting in his pants I saw that he was beyond hard and pulsing as well.

"Finally, when I was shaking and trembling and crying profusely like a goddamned schoolgirl my two buddies stopped beating my ass cheeks," Hector told us as he went on with his story. "They put their belts back on, stepped behind me, and like two faggots began squeezing and kneading my red wounded ass cheeks. Shit man, I never had any guys squeezing my big butt before. They pulled me up off the table and turned me around.

I stood there crying, sweating, and moaning in pain as they ran their mangy hands over me everywhere. Richard asked me if I was glad that I had decided to along with his idea for the loser of the game. I just looked at him in total misery; it was a look of disbelief that was on my face actually. Then, to further add to my shock my two buddies leaned down and slurped my big nips into their greedy fucking mouths. Shit, I had been working with these guys for more than a year or so at that point and never once did I think that they could be faggots.

I called them faggots, swore at them, and realized how I had been had. They had hoped upon hope that I would lose the damned card game. Bob told me that one didn't have to be a faggot to enjoy a great tasting pair of sweaty nipples. Fuck, they slurped, sucked, nursed on and chewed my nips like crazy. No girl I ever dated ever treated my nips like that. I would suppose that was what made my cock get hard. I was a mess of goose bumps and chills and thrills as my two good buddies really put the screws to my nips more and more. When Richard noticed my hard pulsing cock he reached down and took the meaty thing in his hand. I gulped loud in disbelief as he began stroking me. Now I knew that my two buddies were faggots. He stroked me and stroked me till I shot what would be the first of many loads. I came like gangbusters, spewing a hefty sized load of creamy ball juice all over the cabin floor, swearing all the while. I grunted, groaned, and swore like a trapped marine as they went on eating my nips, making me shoot my load. I have to admit though that there is something tantalizing about being made to shoot your load when you really don't want to.

When I was done spewing my mess my two buddies went on eating my nips like crazy. It was then that I realized just how sensitive a guy's nipples can become after shooting his load. I screamed and begged for them to stop but they were relentless those two buddies of mine. I got the feeling that they had planned this for a long time and now I was in no goddamned position to stop them. As sweat poured off me they went on slurping heartily at my nipples like two bitches in heat, like their very lives depended on it. I curled my toes back under my socks as my nipples began to feel numb and overly erect on my chest. As they slurped at them they slapped my pecs hard, really getting some good squeals out of me, fuck, I sounded like a stuck pig. Then, Bob reached down and took my slimy cum coated semi hard cock in his hand and began stroking and choking me a second time.

Let me tell you I really fucking panted at that point. I could not believe that half of this was even happening, and that it had begun no less. A feeling of total helplessness enveloped me as my two buddies ate my nipples and Bob stroked me toward gusher number two. It didn't take all that long to get me fully hard again as the way they were slurping the fuck out of my nips was at that point making me nuts. Bob stroked me slow, fast, and slow again. Twice when I felt myself getting close to shooting my second load he would stop stroking me and make me *not* cum. God, that was awful, but then finally he fisted my cock tightly in his hand and stroked me till I shot another good sized construction worker load.

Again, I grunted and swore like a damned marine as I spewed my mess all over the cabin floor. As I came the second time they didn't once let up on my poor nipples. Fuck, but, I was in agony for sure then. Every part of me was alive and tingling, except for my nips that is. They were numb in my buddies' mouths.

Hector fell silent for a second to take a few good deep breaths as he hung there from the tree branch.

"Say, you guys think I could have more water before I go on?" he asked us politely.

"Sure thing Muscle boy," Ronald said and put his canteen to Hector's lips.

As Hector sipped the water I again hunkered down at his sweaty sore cock and balls. As soon as he was done drinking I slurped his soft and shriveled cock into my mouth as Ronald went to work on one of his nipples again with his mouth, teasing his other nipple with his fingers.

"OHHHHHRRRRRR, fucking fucked up guys just can't stop feasting on me!" Hector grunted miserably.

I sucked him till his poor cock was painfully hard in my mouth. Ronald ran a hand all over the muscle guy's sweat soaked chest, sending chills through him at what must have felt like a hundred miles an hour. I caressed Hector's strong muscular legs as his cock pounded like a thing alive in my mouth.

"Ohhhhhhhhh man, getting me there again you slimy fuckers!" he seethed. "Good God and all his angels, but I'm going to be beyond exhausted by the time this fucked up day is over!" I gave his sore cock a few more good sucks and slurps and then the muscle boy announced breathlessly that he was cumming for what felt like the thousandth time that day.

"Ohhhhhrrrrr!!!" he roared mostly in pain as I held his cock in my hand.

Only a small spurt of clear cum slithered out of his cock. As he stood there catching his breath Ronald and I took our mouths off him.

"Okay bud, tell us what happened after your two work buddies stopped eating your great big tits," Ronald said with authority in his voice.

Hector looked at us miserably and said that he was going to get us for this, for all of this. He however at the moment went on with his story.

"After what seemed like forever those two perverted buddies of mine stopped torturing my damned nips," Hector said as he caught his breath. "My poor nips were swollen to the size of two cherries on my chest and they were numb and tingling. Bob then told me that they were going to take me for a walk in the woods just the way I was, balls ass naked. I ranted at him how that was totally out of the question, but I really wasn't in much of a position to resist. Before taking me out of the cabin and making me walk in just my socks through the woods my two buddies decided that I needed more whips to my ass. Can you believe that shit? They had already whipped my poor butt cheeks good and fucking red, but now I was in for more... They took turns holding me over their laps and spanking the fuck out of my poor ass cheeks with wooden spoons. Like I said, it wasn't bad enough that they'd whipped the hell out of my cheeks earlier with their belts, but now they were walloping me with wooden spoons. With my arms trussed tightly up behind me, I was totally at their mercy as they took their turns holding me across their laps the way my father used to do to me. By the time they stopped walloping me with those wooden spoons I was a sniveling crying mess. My ass cheeks were burning and stinging miserably. They stood me up between them and Bob held me by my upper arms as Richard again began stroking my big tube steak. Fucking guy wanted me to shoot another damned load, and from all points I would."

As Hector spoke Ronald had stepped behind him and was again squeezing and kneading his luscious ass cheeks.

"Man oh fucking man, I could just take a bight out of these sexy cheeks of his," Ronald exclaimed, his hands filled with the silky flesh.

"Hey come on you guys, let me finish my story here," Hector panted as I joined Ronald behind the muscle boy and gave his big ass cheeks a few hard squeezes myself. "That way when I'm done you two can cut me down and I'll get on my way."

Ronald and I looked at each other, snickered, and we each gave the muscle boy's ass cheeks a hard slap. He yelped in pain and went on with his story.

"Yeah, anyway, where the fuck was I?" Hector asked. "Oh yeah, that bastard Richard was stroking my tube steak again, getting me closer to shooting a third load for him and Bob. I stood there between them feeling pretty miserable and utterly humiliated. I mean, how often does a guy get stripped to his socks, tied up, have his ass whipped and then get jacked off by his two good buddies? It took a while longer but I did shoot a third load, right onto the cabin floor. It mixed with the mess of my cum that was already on the floor. Jeez, from all the goop of mine that was on the floor anyone seeing it would have thought that a few guys had jacked off in that cabin. I came in a mixture of pleasure and pain that time and realized quite awfully that if they kept jacking me off it would become more painful each time. But what the fuck could I do to stop them? When I was done shooting my third load my two buddies squatted down in front of me and they each slurped one of my big juicy and sweaty balls into their mouths. That really fucking blew my mind let me tell you…"

"Now that sounds like a plan to me," Ronald blurted eagerly and in seconds he and I were hunkered down in front of the trapped muscle boy.

"Ohhhhhhhhrrrrr no, no, not my goddamned balls you guys, *please!!!*" Hector gasped as we ignored him and each of us gobbled one of his plum sized nuts into our mouths. "Ohhhhhhhhhrrrrr fucking shit, I'll fucking kill Richard and Bob when I get back to that cabin!!"

Ronald and I snickered softly with Hector's balls in our mouths, both of us knowing that the guy would not be going back to the cabin for some time yet. We really put the screws to his poor balls, sucking them hard, applying maddening pressure to them with the tips of our tongues, and even yanking them down hard with our mouths. Hector screamed and grunted in a real man's pain, swearing like a captured marine all over again, and at the same time begging for release in between. The muscle boy's big balls were all sweaty and smelly and they tasted like a real fucking guy's balls. The scents of his piss and cum assaulted our taste buds as we feasted on heartily on Hector's nuts. When his balls were good and swollen we stopped sucking them and got to our feet. The poor guy was sniveling and crying like a kid, tears rolling down his face.

"Bastards, *bastards,* you're as bad as those two perverted buddies of mine," Hector snorted angrily. "It's not bad enough that my two buddies worked me over like crazy, but now I have you two perving all over me!"

We each gave his huge pecs a hard slap and then Ronald asked him what Richard and Bob did to him after they had sucked the fuck out of his balls. Hector managed to get himself under some sort of control and then went on to tell us of how his two buddies milked his cock a fourth time before taking him for a horrendous walk in the woods.

"I tell you, those two so called buddies of mine just loved jacking the fuck out of my cock," Hector said angrily. "After they had sucked my poor balls to the point of agony Bob took another turn at milking me. I stood there between them in utter misery. I mean, good as it may feel how often is it that a guy has two of his buddies milking him of his loads over and over? It took a while for Bob to get my cock jacked up and hard due to the pain my balls were in, not to mention my red striped butt cheeks. I guess I was concentrating more on the pain than the pleasure I was feeling. As Bob stroked me I realized how sore my cock was starting to become. Being repeatedly jacked off is not all that much fun let me tell you. I was sweating, feeling lousy and wishing that I had kept my big yap shut when Richard had suggested the consequences for the loser of the game. Actually, if I were in a position to choose I would rather have stayed in that cabin being milked like a cow over and over rather than being brought out here and left hanging from a goddamned tree branch. But I wasn't in a position to choose and I knew that once I shot that fourth load for them my two buddies were going to be taking me for a horrible romp in the woods. Bob stroked me and stroked me like a madman until my cock was good and hard again. Now trust me you two clowns, I'm fucking straight as a goddamned arrow so don't think that just because that buddy of mine was stroking me I got hard. I don't give a rat's ass who's jacking your cock; you're going to lay a boner no matter what! Once I was hard my cock pulsed in numbing agony in Bob's hand as Richard squeezed my shoulder, leaned over me, and slurped one of my sore nips into his greedy mouth. I grunted from my throat and found that I was gyrating myself as my two buddies feasted on me more and more. I thought how we would have a lot to talk about in a few days. Then, as I was sucked and stroked like crazy I felt myself getting close to shooting that fourth load for them. The sounds of sucking and my slimy cock being stroked filled the cabin. This time I tried my best to hold it back for as long as possible, knowing what was going to happen after I came this time. But then, Bob stroked me faster and faster and harder and harder and Richard slurped like crazy on my nipple. There was no holding back at that point. Exhausted as I was, and still am, I shot a small spurt of cum for them, groaning breathlessly as Bob stroked every damned droplet out of me. I screeched like a madman as Richard went on slurping my nipple, bighting the tip of it with his front teeth. I pleadingly begged him to stop. Fuck guys, every time I shot my damned load my poor nips became more and more sensitive. *That* shit can make a poor guy crazy that is for sure. When Richard stopped torturing my nipple I stood there again catching my breath as my two buddies began gathering up their backpacks and filling them with things to take on a walk through the woods. I fucking begged them not to do this, not to make me walk with them through the woods in just my damned socks. I told Richard that this was definitely taking things, and me, too far, but the bastard ignored me. Standing there watching them I tried desperately to get my arms untied, but it was no use. I was tied too damned tight. After Richard and Bob were dressed in fatigue style pants, hiking boots, tee shirts, and their backpacks slung over their backs they were ready. I on the other hand was anything but ready. My ass cheeks were stinging and in pain, my nipples had been chewed to the size of ripe cherries and my cock and balls were sore beyond the fact. Richard gave me a good cool drink of water from his canteen and then we were ready to go. I made sure to thank him for the drink because I thought I wouldn't be getting any water till it was all over. Couldn't have me dehydrating though could they? I mean, this was mean fun they were having with me but if a guy is thirsty you can't deny him a cool drink."

Hector stopped speaking for a moment as Ronald gave him some water.

"Th-thanks man," Hector said to Ronald and then went on. "Bob checked to make sure that no one was around outside before we left the cabin. From the doorway he told Richard and I that the coast was clear. Richard, standing behind me told me to get moving. I turned and looked at him helplessly, silently begging him not to do this. With a slap on my ass he got me moving. The three of us exited the cabin and my two buddies quickly hustled me into the woods, each of them holding me by one of my upper arms. I swore at them all over again but damn it all, it had no effect. When we were in the woods and completely out of sight of being caught Richard told Bob to stop walking for a moment. He told him that he had a really mean and twisted idea in mind for me. He opened his backpack and took out a length of rope. In moments rope was tied snugly around my balls. Richard held the length of rope in his hand, pulling on it as I walked ahead of him and Bob. Richard pulled the rope back so far that my poor balls were pushed hard against my damned ass crack. I yelled angrily to Richard that this was beyond twisted, this was outright lunacy and a lousy fucked up thing to do to a guy you called your buddy. After we had been walking for about fifteen minutes or so my socks were filthy and stinking. I was covered and matted in sweat, and mosquitoes and flies were having a grand time taking bights out of me. Then, Richard pulled really hard on the rope tied around my balls and said whoa. I instantly stopped walking. Bob gave me some water and then he and Richard hunkered down in front of me. The two perverts took turns this time sucking my cock. Richard said that whoever had my cock in his mouth when I shot my load this time would get to hold the rope around my balls when we walked on. Needless to say I was not enjoying having my pride and joy sucked by two guys who were my friends. Shit, I didn't want *any fucking guy* sucking my cock. I clenched my teeth as they took turns running their lips over the sides of my sore cock. Unbelievably I was hard within a few minutes. Bob won the prize. I was in his mouth when I shot my load that time. Fucking guy man, he ate my sperm like it was the best thing he ever tasted. As he gulped down the small spurt that erupted from my wide sexy slit Richard meanly pulled on the rope tied around my balls. I yelped in pain, as the woods seemed to spin in front of me. When I was done Bob let my cock slip out of his mouth. He and Richard stood up. Richard smoothed my sweat-drenched hair back and told me reassuringly that I was doing very well. I sarcastically thanked him. Bob took the rope in hand and told me to get moving. With my poor cock smarting and dangling semi hard in front of me I walked on in front of my two buddies. Bob pulled meanly on the rope, yanking my balls up and under my ass crack again. I plodded through mud holes, endured insects crawling on me everywhere, and even being bitten by those insects. I prayed that they wouldn't make me walk through any poison ivy. I mean fuck, I didn't need to be laid up with that. After another good half-hour or so of endless walking Richard suggested stopping again and milking me a few more times. I gulped in total disbelief at his words. I could not possibly be made to shoot a few loads at that point. But that was not up to me to find out if it was possible or not. It was at that point that my two buddies untied my arms and before I could do any damned thing they had my wrists pulled above my head and tied. The slack of the rope they tied up to the branch of this tree. The only consolation I have is that they took the damned rope off my balls."

"And you've been here ever since?" I asked the trapped muscle boy.

"Since they were here and since they milked two more loads of my good stuff from me," Hector said miserably. "That last load they got from me was downright awful. Fuck man, all I felt was a tingling in the tip of my meat stick. Nothing came out. I was shooting dry orgasms by then. And it was true, that could drive a poor schmuck of a guy crazy."

Ronald and I looked at each other, a knowing look in our eyes. We had milked the muscle boy a few times ourselves, *but* we were sure we could get more out of him, but not here in the middle of the woods. And milking him was just one of the things we intended to get from him.

"Did they tell you how long they planned to keep you out here sweating for?" Richard asked Hector and squeezed one of his nipples hard.

"Just long enough to torment me and to make me sweat my guts out a lot more," Hector replied. "I begged them not to leave me here, telling them that I would do anything if they would just fucking untie me. To keep me from attracting any unwanted attention and to stop the screaming I had done while shooting that last load and just to keep me quiet while they took a few last sucks on my nipples that bastard Richard gagged me. Then I watched in utter misery as they walked off back to the cabin. And believe me; they are not going to be happy to see you two pawing me."

"That's what we figured as well muscle boy," I said. "Which is why we will untie you, but we're not going to let you go all that quickly. You see, we're staying in a cabin that a friend of mine gave us the key to, and it's on the other side of the woods from where you and your two buddies are staying."

Hector gulped loudly and a look of outright fear mixed with disbelief came over his gorgeous face.

A few moments later Ronald had climbed up the tree to the branch that the slack of the rope around Hector's wrists was tied to. We had tied the muscle boy's socked feet together real tightly at the ankles with some rope that Ronald had in his backpack, preventing him from running off when the slack of the rope was freed from the branch.

"Okay Alex, as soon as I untie this grab his bound wrists," Ronald said loudly down to me. "I don't want muscle boy trying anything."

"Not to worry Ronald my man," I replied up to him. "I doubt he's in any shape to be doing anything except what we tell him to."

"Come on man, give me a fucking break here!!" Hector panted pleadingly to me, looking at me and glancing up at Ronald as he undid the knots in the ropes around the tree branch. "You have to let me go!! Please man!!!"

Not wanting to be distracted I took the gag from around Hector's neck, crammed the front of it back into his mouth, and tied it tightly behind his head. He looked at me with eyes filled with utter despair and nodded his head "no" from side to side, the prospect of being kidnapped this way obviously terrifying him. He made a few moaning sounds from behind his gag as I watched intently as Ronald untied the rope around the branch. When the rope was freed from the branch Hector was finally able to lower his numb and aching muscular arms.

"MMMMFFFF!!!!" he sputtered like a madman and tried unsuccessfully to pull his bound wrists away from my waiting grasp.

I held tightly to Hector's bound wrists as he tottered stupidly on his tied feet, trying to pull away from me. Ronald made his way down quickly from the tree branch to help me. When Ronald hit the ground he and I quickly pressed Hector's bound wrists up against his chest and tied the long slack of the rope around and around his bent arms, pinning his muscular arms to his body.

"RRRRRMMMMFFFFF!!!" he roared beyond angrily, saliva spewing out of the sides of his gagged mouth.

"Yeah, I'm sure I know just how you feel you poor kid," I said merrily as I trussed the guy up tight.

Moments later Hector was standing between Ronald and I, all packaged and ready to go. I can't tell you what a sight he made as he tried desperately to balance himself on his tied up smelly socked feet. Suddenly, from not too far off in the distance we heard Hector's name being called out. Ronald and I looked at each other in total alarm.

"Yo Hector!!! It's us buddy, Richard and Bob!! We're coming to get you guy!!" we heard a voice calling out loudly. "I bet by now you're all ready to be cut down huh guy?"

"RRRRmmmmmmmffffff!!!" Hector called out helplessly to his two buddies who were still pretty far off.

"Let's get the fuck out of here!" Ronald said, pulling his backpack over his shoulder and grabbing Hector's upper arms in his big hands. "Grab his stinking feet Alex!!"

I quickly hauled my backpack onto my shoulder and did as Ronald said. A look of confusion mixed with terror spread over the tied and gagged muscle boy's handsome face as we hoisted him up off the ground between us.

"Thought we were going to leave you behind after all huh Muscle boy?" I asked him.

"Hey Hector!! Can you hear us?" another voice called out as we walked off at a fast pace with our load between us.

"RRRRmmmmmffff…" Hector whimpered pitifully.

By the time Richard and Bob got to the tree where they had left their muscle boy buddy tied up and gagged all they found was some cum on the ground. They looked around but thanks to the fact that the ground was dry and strewn with leaves we had not left any footprints when we carried Hector off with us. The two construction workers stupidly guessed that their buddy had gotten himself loose, jacked off a few times, and then made his way back to their cabin on his own. They had no idea whatsoever that two guys had come along and snatched their handsome and helpless hunky buddy.

Quirks

About the Author

Christopher Trevor was born in July 1963 and grew up in New York City. As soon as he was old enough to know how he began writing fiction and has been writing gay erotic/fetish stories for the past ten to twelve years at this point. He became an avid reader as well from the time he knew how and reads everything from fiction, to non-fiction to biographies of interesting and unusual people, people who have made a difference or who have paved the way for others. Christopher attributes his writing artistic inspiration to artists such as Etienne, Tom of Finland, Tagame, The Hun, and most notably Joe T, who Christopher has had the pleasure of speaking with and even meeting over the last few years. Christopher states, "Joe T encouraged me to write about my fetish because I was embarrassed about it at the time. Joe T said that when we are embarrassed about something that makes it even more enticing somehow." Christopher totally agreed and never stopped writing in this genre. Erotic writers who inspired Christopher Trevor were: Tom Shaw (author of "That Day at the Quarry), C.S. White (author of Big Sur), Larry Townsend (author of countless erotic novels), and Mason Powell (author of the classic story "The Brig.")

Christopher discovered that not only did he enjoy writing erotic tales but that after his first bondage experience he had a genuine flair for it. Writing to erotic oriented magazines about his first bondage experience truly opened the floodgates for Christopher where this style of writing is concerned. Christopher thanks the handsome and muscular "Greg" for that experience way back in time. Christopher took "Creative Writing" courses every semester during his high school years and while other friends of his stopped writing what they loved to write about as time went on Christopher never let a day go by when he didn't write something… "I feel that if I don't write every day I will die," Christopher has said many times over.

Foot fetish stories and all things related; spanking fetish, erotic shaving, muscle bondage, tickle torture, and hardcore stories are just a few of the areas of gay eroticism that Christopher enjoys writing about and inspiring in others as well. As one internet buddy said to Christopher where the black socks fetish is concerned, "Until I started talking with you I never gave a thought to my socks when I got dressed for work in the morning. Now when I pull my dress socks on every morning I get a chill up my spine."

Christopher is proud of the erotic effect he has on people…

Christopher Trevor is also the author of:

The Executive Guide to Foot Fetishism and Office Discipline
1-887895-36-1

Executive Ties That Bind
1-887895-37-X

Don't!! Stop!! That Tickles!!
1-887895-31-0

The Taming of Dominick
1-887895-45-0

Timmy and The Hong Kong Tailor
1-887895-30-2

Love, Torture and Redemption
1-887895-32-9

Timmys Ticklish Trials
978-1-887895-74-3

The Gym Instructor
978-1-887895-44-6

Milked
978-1-887895-66-8

Erotic Street Blues
978-1-887895-97-2

The Abusive Wager
978-1-887895-04-0

Terry's Appointment and Other Tickling Stories
978-1-934625-08-8

The Military File
978-1-934625-21-7

Look for them where you bought this book or Goodboner.com.

www.ingramcontent.com/pod-product-compliance
Lightning Source LLC
Chambersburg PA
CBHW071231260626
47162CB00004B/1519